Her Heart

Mary L. Schmidt

Her Heart
Mary L. Schmidt

Copyright © 2021
by Mary Schmidt (M. Schmidt Productions)
All rights reserved

Cover design by Mary L. Schmidt

BISAC Subject Headings:
Fiction /Indigenous
Fiction / Romance / Contemporary
Fiction / Indigenous Peoples of the Americas
Library of Congress
ISBN- 978-0-578-97280-0 Paperback
ISBN-13: 978-0-578-97281-7 Ebook

First edition published August 2021

Blog (https://www.whenangelsfly.net)
Facebook (https://www.facebook.com/MMSchmidtAuthorGDDonley)
Twitter (https://twitter.com/MaryLSchmidt)
Deviant Art (http://mschmidtartwork.deviantart.com/)

Dedication

Always to Shane, and Sammy, who taught us so much about life, bravery, and that a baby and a five-year-old can be wiser beyond their brief time on Earth,

Always to Gene, our son, who we cherish so much, and has been wise beyond his years, and has turned into a kind man,

Always to Michael, my beloved husband, partner, and best friend in the entire world,

Always to Mary, my beloved wife, partner, and best friend in the entire world.

Contents

Prologue

Visions of her Cherokee grandmother, Cordie, flashed through Sarah's mind as her abusive husband brutally raped her repeatedly shortly after giving birth. He took what he wanted, leaving her bloody body to be filled with years of physical pain and emotional scars that led her to believe she was worthless, and a happy life was hopeless. Sarah tried many times to leave but that was always futile. She felt useless. Her life was shattered once again when her oldest son, John, died at birth and Simon, her youngest endured a horrific cancer battle. With her only living son, Daniel, she felt renewed strength knowing Cordie was watching over them always. She finally had the courage with the help of Cordie's visions from the spirit world to leave her abusive husband and make a new life for her and her son. Her new oath to her and Daniel was that no one would ever hurt either of them. Romantic love never existed for Sarah, although she had room in her heart for love. Life taught her to be wary, until the day an old friend from her past, Aaron, came back into her life. Would she finally find and know true love? Could Aaron break through the walls that surrounded her? Dare she hope for love once?

Chapter One

Sarah

"Romantic love never existed for Sarah, although she had room in her heart for love. Life taught her to be wary, until the day an old friend from her past, Aaron, came back into her life. Would she finally find and know true love? Could Aaron break through the walls that surrounded her? Dare she hope for love once?"

Cocooned in the small two-bedroom apartment I shared with my son, Danny, in Lakewood, Colorado, I felt unexposed to the risks of everyday life, particularly men. At age 30, I retreated inside my small shell and allowed a few trusted friends inside with me and Danny. My wavy blond hair cascaded over my shoulders and down my back, showing off a trim, slim figure in denim capri pants, an old T-shirt, and brown leather sandals – all five foot three inches of me. Danny was eight now, with short darker hair and cobalt blue eyes he received from me, and he loved going to school and playing with friends, yet he always spent most of his time at home. After the horrific loss of his baby brother, and my youngest son, Simon, from the effects of treating aggressive cancer, Danny was lonely.

I realized my son needed to be socially connected to others his age and enrolling him in the Boy Scout Program was the perfect way for Danny to reintegrate socially into society. I made sure to be involved in the scouting program as much as possible, so I never worked Monday evenings.

Working as a registered nurse on the trauma unit of a level one hospital, gave me a chance to help others in the milieu of the world of medicine, and I was fulfilling my passion as I cared for my patients. I'd made friends with some of the staff, and adored caring for my patients. Getting back into a working pattern after Simon died was no easy task, as I'd lived day and night at his bedside for eight months. With support from co-workers, particularly my best friend, Suzy Hill, another registered nurse, I was determined to restart my life with Daniel while protecting my heart and soul.

Chin up and have faith, things come in threes... I thought to myself as my Cherokee Indian grandmas' spirit whispered.

I'd been close with Grandma Cordie. We were thick. Sadly, I lost her right after Danny was born, a heart attack took Cordie into the spiritual realm.

Later, after Danny had his bath and was fast asleep, I fell into a restless sleep, and words viciously yelled at me by my ex slipped into my dreams. *You are nothing… you have 'nubbins' for breasts… hee… you are only a sperm receptacle… no man wants you… as he slammed my body into the kitchen wall knocking my head through the plaster and slats…in front of my son… before leaving to drink beer and have sex with women he picked up in the nearby bar.*

"No. Please stop kicking me! Don't hurt me! No! No…!" spilled from my mouth in my dream state of terror. Danny was yelling and shaking my arm.

"Mom! Wake up! You're okay. He can't hurt you anymore. Please Mom!"

Opening my eyes, I saw Danny looking at me with cobalt eyes of terror filled with tears. "I'm sorry. I had a bad dream, I'm sorry that I scared you and woke you up. Come snuggle in bed with me, Danny."

"I remember what Dad did to you. I saw you get

thrown into the kitchen wall and I won't forget it, ever!" Danny yelled.

After a deep breath, I gently spoke with soft words. "I'm so sorry you saw and remember that incident. I'm so sorry that both you and Simon saw this kind of cruelty your entire lives. The abuse will never happen again, not ever, and I love you and cherish you, Danny," I promised as my son crawled into my bed next to me and we soon fell back asleep.

As a young child, I watched "*Julia*" on television. That character was played by Diahann Carroll, and she was compassionate with patients. Widowed, Julia raised the young son alone. My role model was always Julia. She had the ideals I looked for in a mother and a nurse. I even had a "Julia" doll when little. No one understood me, it was me in a world of my own, helping kids, just trying to emulate my favorite television nurse, and reading. I would get lost in any type of book and pretend I was *Nancy Drew* or *Laura Ingalls Wilder*.

My father was in heaven now. My mother, who was an evil bitter woman, lived in a different state from Danny and me. I missed my dad and his wise teachings. My mother had ghosted us, and I was fine with that. It was for the best. I'd never want Danny to be influenced by such an evil and malicious person.

I was an attentive nurse not above shedding a tear with a patient or family… professional, yet consoling, strong yet human with my patients and family. It made no sense to me that I could be positive about my professional skills and downright self-conscious about my looks and body. I was damaged goods,' and no man would see me as anything else. Neither did I want any man thinking of me in that way. From here on out it would be Danny and me.

Dark shadows were evident under my eyes the next morning, but I wanted to be cheerful when Danny woke up. Attempts to camouflage my dark circles with makeup, and red eyes with eye drops failed miserably. I was a complete failure at marriage, yet I wanted to be the best mom I could be for Danny. Danny never lacked for love and attention, and I never once spanked that little bottom of his. He didn't get away with doing something he knew not to do—I simply employed other methods of reprimand.

Danny came bouncing into the kitchen after the scent of bacon had wafted down the hall and through the open bedroom door. "Are you hungry this morning? Take a seat. Breakfast is ready", I replied as I greeted Danny with a hug and kiss. "Orange juice or chocolate milk this morning?"

"I want both, Mom. I'm starving! You make the best breakfast and I love you," Danny spoke with a huge smile showing one tooth missing – a baby tooth – and a permanent tooth barely visible. Danny's smile always warmed my heart and his charming little dimples melted me.

Smiling at my son, I declared, "I love you, too, Danny. I love you big, huge, ginormous bunches!" Then I kissed the top of his head.

After dropping him off at school, I made my way to work. It was nice that my nursing schedule allowed for me to be home in the early mornings and back home by 6 p.m. The trauma center was busy, and I split my time between placing PICC's (peripherally inserted central catheters) and the trauma unit. Time flew by each day, and I was grateful, for I didn't have time to dwell on dark thoughts of past events.

The last year had been hard for Danny at school. When Simon was sick, Danny's brain didn't focus on schoolwork. The last thing I expected was a call from the school wanting to set up a visit with Miss Gale, a teacher, and other staff. The secretary didn't elucidate on the reason for this meeting except to say that Danny struggled. I was to be there at nine in the morning. Luckily, this worked into my schedule.

Chapter Two

Sarah

One year ago…

Danny had been hurt when my husband beat him. He tried to strangle Danny! It was time! It was past time. Grandma Cordie's Cherokee strength flowed into me, and I quietly asked Danny if he wanted to live in a different home, away from the abuse. "Danny, do you want to move out, to find a new home?" He sobbed into my blouse and begged me to move us out of our house of hell. Through heavy painful sobs, he begged to leave right then and there.

"Okay, Danny, we will. Now stay with me while I pack." I murmured to my son while I stuffed clothing and favorite toys into four suitcases, and we crept from the house to my Jeep. Buckled into our seats with doors locked, I backed out of the garage for the last time.

First, I took Danny to the emergency room to

have his ribs and head checked out. Dr. Aaron Leawood, a friend since high school, was Danny's ER doctor. I was ashamed of myself. Had I moved out even one week before, Danny wouldn't be here now. Head CT came back normal, but Danny had a broken clavicle and two broken ribs. I was livid. How could a man do this to his child?

Holding Danny, I murmured, "Danny, you will heal and be okay. I promise never to let that man hurt you ever again. I promise." And I cuddled my sobbing son.

Dr. Aaron Leawood asked me if I wanted to file a police report. Nodding my head yes, the police came in and I filled out the necessary forms. The officer asked Danny if he had anything to add to the report and he said yes. As Danny spilled his guts about abuse that I had no idea happened, I wanted to kill that man – Danny's father – the perpetrator! It would be a cold day in hell before he came near my son again!

Dr. Leawood filled out the paperwork required, and pictures of Danny's injuries were taken by the nurse on duty, Suzy Hill, my friend, and co-worker.

"The reports will help protect you both in court. You are filing for divorce, right?" Dr. Leawood asked.

I nodded in the affirmative.

Luckily, it was a Saturday night, and I booked our hotel room for a full week. I arranged to have a leave of absence from work —two weeks— enough time to get settled in a rental apartment, file for divorce, and for Danny to start the healing process.

The divorce went fast as I wanted no child support and full custody. Both were granted to me. Danny's father moved across the country, then to China, and not a single person has heard a word from him since.

Danny and I started going back to my beloved church, St. Mary's Queen of the Universe, and Danny became an altar boy.

Chapter Three

Danny

One year ago…

I liked my school, my teacher, Miss Gale, and I especially liked math and geography. I had trouble working out the reading type of math problems, not one made sense to me. Math should be numbers only. Miss Gale said that mom would be here tomorrow morning for a meeting. I wondered what it was about. Some of my grades were bad, and I hoped I would not get into trouble or anything bad!

Mom wanted me to read more books and I did— when she was around. If mom was busy cooking or cleaning, I snuck my Ninja Turtles out from under my bed, and soon I was taking care of Ninja Turtle stuff all over the city of Lakewood, Colorado. I was Raphael! Simon and I played with our Ninja Turtles before sickness and heaven happened. I liked not seeing Simon in pain and decided I would have

Donatello, the smallest Ninja Turtle, play with Raphael. Simon had loved Donatello, and we had placed a stuffed Donatello in the casket before he was buried.

"What would you like for dinner, Danny?" Mom called out.

"Meatloaf and fried potatoes with peas," I yelled from my bedroom. Mom made the best meatloaf! Mom cooked one of my favorite meals almost every day. On days mom's eyes showed tiredness, we would grab fast food—chicken nuggets with honey and fries were my favorite. Mom was a busy nurse at work.

I was excited to start with the Boy Scouts, and I loved scouting. Tommy Carson became my friend and I made other friends, too. The adventures we had working on badges towards becoming an Eagle Scout were lots of fun. My love of nature grew, and I was busy doing many projects with the other scouts, yet I was sad that Simon couldn't join in. At age six, Simon's death had hurt me badly. I was still sad a lot of the time, especially when I wasn't involved in doing homework or with my friends or mom. Now, I was eight and the man of the house, so I cried less at night. My new scouting friend, Nathan Eastman, did the best he could to help when I was sad. Tommy and Nathan didn't understand why I was still sad about losing Simon, but they invited me to their houses to play and have fun, as I was an 'only' child now. Mom let me have Tommy and Nathan at our apartment, too. Mom would make up games and stories if we asked, and we three boys had lots of ideas of our own. Our family room was gigantic, and mom let us set up a tent to use as a fort—no moms allowed. We lived in a safe neighborhood, in a second-floor brick apartment building. It was nice, and we had a swimming pool, exercise room, and tennis courts included—if you lived in our building, you could use the nice facilities.

"Time to eat, young man," Mom called out. I ran to the table, ready for meatloaf. Yum. Mom made cherry pie for dessert. I remembered how Simon always loved to eat this meal, too. Simon ate everything he could get a hand on. I liked my memories, but they also made me sad, sometimes.

After dinner, Mom asked me if I wanted to go shoot some hoops with her at the fitness center connected to the hospital she worked at. "Yes, please! Let's go have fun!"

The fitness center was always busy, and Mom found one end of a court for us to play alone. We played ball and I beat Mom in baskets and dribbles! "I think you need to try harder, Mom, if you want to catch up with me," I stated as she tackled me down onto a gym mat and tickled me. I was laughing so much that people looked over to see what the fuss was about. Many of them laughed with us. After the game, Mom treated me to an ice cream cone.

Later, as I fell asleep, I was smiling as I remembered the excitement of the basketball game. I wished that Simon had been there. I'm a big boy now—the man of the house, so I didn't cry myself to sleep. I was still sad, and I wanted to cry, but I didn't.

Chapter Four

Aaron

At age 33, I was a complete failure in the marriage department. During medical school, my first wife left me. Then, my new girlfriend got pregnant, so for my daughter's sake, we married, and I tried to make the marriage work. That marriage was doomed from the start, though, and my second wife left shortly after our daughter, Lisa, was born.

Women!

Women wanted meal tickets and an easy life. Clubbing was the wrong way to meet women who didn't want me for what I could offer as a well-respected doctor here in the city. Every day, patients and co-workers hit on me, constantly trying to capture a well-respected doctor. It was tiring, but the more I ignored them, the harder they tried. Such was the way of hospital life. With two marriages down the tubes, I decided to focus on my job and my daughter,

Lisa, for now. Dressed in green scrubs with my dark curly hair under a scrub cap, I made my way to the trauma unit as I heard my name being paged overhead.

Good morning, doctor," Sarah greeted me. "We have a thirteen-year-old boy who fell off a ski lift and sustained a compound fracture of his right leg along with head trauma. He was taken down the run by a rescue team on a snowmobile and transferred to the ambulance. ETA is minutes." The ambulance bay doors opened, and I started barking orders.

"Put the patient in room three and page neuro and ortho now!" I ordered. "Nice stabilization of the leg," he told the EMS workers. "Any problems during the ride?" I asked as I assessed the child.

"I want a head CT stat! First a head CT and then full x-rays of the leg," I barked.

"Yes, doctor," Sarah responded, working efficiently. I input the orders in the computer as I called for a stat head CT. I prayed for no brain damage. Neuro assessed the boy as they headed for the CT scanner. CT was clear, but neuro said they would follow the teenager while in hospital. Ortho took over then to treat the compound fracture of the right leg. The parents were informed of what was happening and why, and both agreed with the plan of care. Ortho had papers signed for surgery and into the operating theater he did go.

Sarah…

As a registered nurse, it is my job to teach parents. Dr. Leawood and I kept the parents informed. Both parents were thankful their son didn't sustain an obvious head injury, but I taught what to look and watch for regarding a concussion, such as extra sleepiness, nausea, confusion, headaches, and problems with concentration, memory, balance, and coordination. The parents were then taken to the surgical waiting room.

Aaron…

After the boy left the ER, Sarah Anderson spoke up "Care for a cup of coffee from Gourmet Supreme? I'm going for their special peppermint hot chocolate. It's so cold outside!" Gourmet Supreme was in the hospital lobby and I was thankful to Sarah for going. "Sure, I'd love my usual cappuccino with an extra shot of espresso. Both the drinks are on me," I replied, handing her a ten-dollar bill.

Sarah had been a friend since high school but was three years younger than me. Life was tough for Sarah. First, her young son died tragically of cancer, and then a messy divorce. I knew the man she'd married only by sight. Sarah changed after her marriage and become withdrawn with everyone except for me and a few close friends. I knew her ex had physically abused her. I'd seen bruises on her arms for Pete's sake! When I mentioned the bruises to her, Sarah clammed up and didn't speak to me for a long time. When another nurse, Suzy Hill, told me that Sarah finally divorced him, I found myself happy for both Sarah and Danny. Danny must be lacking for a father figure in his life now. The thought of a boy with no father yanked on my heart strings. Maybe I could be a Big Brother to him in my free time. Working in the trauma center didn't leave a lot of that, but it would be time well spent to help a friend and her son.

"Yum, that smells great, Sarah," I said as I took my cappuccino and sipped. I was rewarded with a half-smile from her. "Does Danny like to play basketball?"

"What?"

"I asked if Danny liked to play basketball." Sarah's face initially showed confusion for a moment, and I wondered if I had transgressed into personal space.

"Danny loves to shoot hoops, and some evenings we play basketball in the employee fitness center. Why do you ask?" Sarah questioned me with wearied blue eyes.

"You're a great mom and role model for your son. With Simon passing away, and the two of you alone, I thought I could play hoops with Danny now and then as a sort of 'Big Brother' figure. What do you think? If I am encroaching on your personal territory, please forgive me. I'd never want to spoil or ruin our friendship, Sarah," I assured her as I watched her face closely for any reaction. "If you agree, then we can arrange to play ball after I pick up Lisa, she is four now, from the hospital daycare center."

"Danny has scouting on Mondays, tomorrow is booked, but Wednesday evening is open. How does that sound?" Sarah responded with a miniscule smile.

"Okay, game on! Wednesday evening, say around 6:30 p.m.? Shall we meet at the fitness center?"

Sarah answered in the affirmative as I closed a chart. I was sure I could make a difference in Danny's life maybe, and possibly Sarah would open up and talk to me the way she used to before her marriage. I wanted to help them both, and my daughter would benefit from having Sarah and Danny in her life. Aside from preschool, my housekeeper, Sadie Edwards, and the daycare center, it was Lisa and me, alone at home. As a single father, and a busy trauma physician, it was impossible for me to try and arrange play dates for Lisa. I tried that once and after being hit on by the girl's mother, I decided I wouldn't be doing it again. Sarah was safe, though, and we'd have a good time together.

Chapter Five

Sarah

One year ago…

I did my best and acted like 'normal' this morning before taking Danny to school. He was less talkative, and I tried in vain to get Danny to tell me what was going on in that adorable head. He was evasive, which was something he had mastered.

Danny waited until we'd arrived at the school before asking me about the meeting.

"Am I in trouble, Mom? Did I do something bad? I'm scared. Do I have to repeat first grade?" he asked in a rush as his fearful eyes searched my face.

"No, Danny, you're not in trouble at all. This is a meeting to see what we can do to help you and your grades improve in a couple of areas. Don't worry, Hun," I responded and gave Danny a quick hug before we got out of my maroon Jeep Grand Cherokee Limited 4x4 SUV. I knew he needed that hug from me and not in front of the other kids. Kids certainly do make fun of peers too often in this world in which we lived.

Once inside, Danny headed for his classroom, and I went to the school office. The secretary was on the phone and motioned for me to sit in a nearby chair. When the call ended, I was ushered into a small meeting room and told that the school counselor, Tammy Lind, would be right in. The school psychologist, the speech language pathologist teacher, and Danny's teacher came in with the school principal. This looked bad and a trepidation washed over me. Introductions made, we all sat down.

Grandma Cordie, be with me and help me feel the strength of your Cherokee spirit.

Miss Gale spoke first. "Mrs. Anderson, as I'm sure you are aware, Danny is having problems keeping up with the kids in his grade in several areas. Our goal is to give Danny a better start in the areas of concern."

Okay, no problem yet, we are okay so far. Went through my brain.

Danny's principle responded, "We have thoroughly gone over all areas of your son's education and problem areas. With that in mind, we want to start

Danny on an IEP. You would be involved in the process."

"Danny is *not* mentally handicapped!" I stated and looked each person in the eye.

Miss Gale addressed me directly, "Mrs. Anderson, may I please explain how this works and the benefits Danny would receive?"

Sighing as my shoulders slumped, I nodded my head in agreement as she passed a large stack of paperwork towards me.

"An IEP stands for Individualized Educational Plan, and that plan is developed to ensure that a child who has a disability identified under the law, and is attending an elementary or secondary educational institution, receives specialized instruction and related services." Miss Gale indicated to my stack of papers.

"Danny will catch up. He lost his brother, and he struggles with parts of his homework, but he is NOT mentally handicapped! He is smart as a whip in math. Explain that!" I countered.

"Mrs. Anderson, may I further elucidate the benefits of an IEP?" Miss Gale queried.

"I'm sorry, please do finish what you have to say as I know, for all of us to be present, I must be missing something and I need to know how to fix the problems," I agreed.

"Danny will benefit from an IEP as it's a written document that describes the educational plan for a student with a disability. The IEP talks about the student's disability, what skills he/she needs to learn, what the student is doing in school this year, what services the school will provide, and where learning will take place," stated Miss Gale.

Miss Gale continued, "Furthermore, an IEP lays out special education instructions, support, and services a student needs to thrive in school. IEPs are part of PreK–12 public education. Plus, at the end of Danny's senior year, the paperwork compiled regarding his educational needs, will help him get into college."

"I sat motionless in a catatonic state while I tried to process what they were saying. Danny is smart, so what am I missing? The school psychologist interrupted my train of thought.

"We realize this is a lot to take in. To qualify for special education services, and an IEP, students must meet two separate criteria. First, they must be formally diagnosed as having a disability. This is defined under the Individuals with Disabilities

Education Act. Danny meets the criteria. He has problems with reading and reading comprehension. He will benefit from working with our speech language pathologist. "We suggest you discuss with Danny's pediatrician the options of medication or behavioral cognitive therapy. As it stands now, we suggest Danny repeat the first grade," she finished.

I was speechless. I never saw this coming! When Miss Gale started to speak again, I held up my hand to stop her. "Let me think." In the end, I agreed to start the process of preparing an IEP for Danny.

The label, on the other hand, I did not agree with at all! Danny was labelled as *'Educably Mentally Handicapped'* I was furious! That label did *not* fit Danny. Why, they couldn't even spell – 'educably.' It wasn't a word that I knew of.

Danny was diagnosed with ADHD and placed on medications to supplement the extra help with schooling. This combination helped settle Danny down and he could focus on the schoolwork at hand. I gave freedom of medicine (medication holiday) to Danny on the weekends. Sometimes, growth is stunted on the medicine prescribed, and I wanted Danny to eat all he could on weekends and school breaks as he needed to grow.

As a registered nurse, I would be remiss at best not to write about medications used to help children with ADHD. I won't suggest, nor will I list medication(s) Danny took. As a parent, you are in control, your decision, you have the steering wheel to help your child as you see fit.

The medication is given for attention deficit hyperactivity disorder. Is it right for your child? You and your doctor must decide. Every child is different and no one method will help your child improve, a combination of methods is best. Not all children react the same way to the various medications used for ADHD.

I gave Danny medicine in the mornings only (so as not to mess with evening sleep patterns), and for Danny, the medication he received decreased the anxiety he felt. With improved social anxiety and ADHD symptoms, such as racing thoughts, loss of concentration, and difficulty staying in his seat at school, Danny functioned like other children.

The downside to not giving Danny medication after school or on weekends, meant he didn't perform well on homework at home or in daycare. Together we decided not to give medicine in the late afternoon and Danny did the best with me as a teacher at home.

Chapter Six

Sarah

This evening we were slated to shoot some hoops with Aaron and Lisa. We both arrived at the daycare center in the hospital at the same time. Aaron was helping a blond, pigtailed, Lisa, collect her coat, hat, and bag as Danny grabbed a backpack and winter coat. The early November temperature had dipped to 30 degrees here in the Colorado foothills, and winter attire was required. Danny and I decided to go have chicken nuggets with honey, fries, and hot chocolate in the main hospital cafeteria to warm us up.

Lisa overheard my conversation with Danny about dinner and begged to come along. "I want chicken nuggets, too, Daddy! Please, can we go? Please?" With arms thrown into the air, Aaron gave in with a chuckle. Lisa was wrapped around that man's little finger, and he couldn't say no.

The four of us ate our dinner and both children

were laughing with excitement. It was pure delight to see Danny laughing and smiling. Lisa was too little to play basketball, but I heard giggles and looked to see Lisa tell Danny that rolling and bouncing balls was lots of fun. I wasn't sure, between the four of us, who had the most fun at dinner. It was perfect seeing Danny out of the shell of protection he put up at times.

After cleaning up our table, placing trays and cutlery in the proper areas, and trash in the bin, it was time for that game, so we headed over to the employee fitness center.

Once there, I took Danny into the family dressing room so we could change into gym shorts. This way I kept an eye on him as I slipped my own shorts on. After witnessing many sexual assault cases come through the trauma center, there was no way I was letting Danny go into the men's changing area alone. When we came out, I watched Lisa while Aaron changed in the men's locker room.

Aaron was tall at six feet, four inches, and he was buff. *How did I not know that? How did I miss seeing that? Why am I even looking at that muscle?* We wore scrubs when working, but evidently, I was too wrapped up in my little world with Danny and never noticed any muscle before. He looked great! Gorgeous, and as I came back to my senses, I remembered my pledge to myself, *No more men for me. Not ever!* I looked up and Aaron was winking at me with a smirk, knowing full well I had been checking out the sinewy muscles and the chiseled chin he sported. I turned my embarrassed red face away and told Danny to go and choose the basketball he wanted us to use, and to grab a smaller ball for Lisa.

How did I not know how chiseled and buff Aaron was? Grandma Cordie, help me shed light on my thoughts please.

Aaron's height made hooking the ball through the basket a breeze, but I could tell when he purposely hit the rim and then bounced the ball off without scoring, and that sent Danny into peals of giggles and laughter. Lisa was happy to roll and bounce a smaller ball and laughed with a soon to be four-year-old eagerness.

"Dr. Aaron, you should try to hook a slam dunk shot. You are tall!" Danny yelled as the blue eyes he sported sparkled and danced.

Danny then turned around and dared Aaron to shoot and make a 3-point shot. Aaron lined up outside the lines of the baseline on the other side of the court while Danny giggled with glee. "I bet you can't do it, Dr. Aaron!" Laughing, Aaron prepared his layup, but before he could throw the ball, Danny shouted.

"Stop! You're taller than me, so to make it fair, you have to get down on your knees, Dr. Aaron." Danny was rolling with laughter and by now, most of the hospital employees had gathered to watch the show. They wanted to see the *good doctor* on his knees. I lost it and busted up laughing too.

Lisa ran to her daddy just as he threw the ball, failing miserably. He turned his sad, brown puppy dog eyes on Danny as he stood, then he scooped up a child in each arm. Walking up to the hoop, I handed the ball to Lisa who made the shot.

This must be how normal families live their lives, I thought as I watched Aaron with the children. This must be how normal families love each other. Guilt settled deep in my heart. I gave Danny love, but I couldn't give him a family.

Aaron had won Danny over without even trying. I was thrilled to see the children happy and to witness Danny 'come alive' with joy once again. Words from Cordie's Cherokee spirit popped into my head, *He is good for you… take a chance… open your heart… live, Sarah, live again.* No. This can't happen and must stop. Aaron is my friend. I want friendship with no strings attached. How could Cordie want me to give more than I am willing to give?

Chapter Seven

Aaron

Last evening had gone smoothly with lots of laughter all around. It was nice to see Sarah looking youthful and happy in her denim shorts, t-shirt, and her soft blonde waves pulled back in a ponytail. Sarah laughed with Danny, and it was an infectious laugh. Sarah could turn anything into a fun time back when we were in high school. Why didn't I remember her sweet, trilling laughter? Then it dawned on me. Sarah hadn't laughed like that since she married her ex. He must have done a real number on her. I was pleased that Lisa and I had been the ones to bring that laughter back to Sarah's lips. I wondered what struggles Danny had witnessed at home. Would Danny live with the memories forever?

I remembered how much pain Danny was in that night in the ER from the broken bones he'd suffered at the hands of that man. No child or adult should have to suffer this way. Sarah did the right thing by bringing Danny to the ER, and then filing a police report with photographs. Both Sarah and Danny had been miserable that night. Sarah had left the soon to be ex and safely ensconced Danny in a hotel room for a week, before moving into a two-bedroom apartment in a nice neighborhood close to the school he attended.

My daughter enjoyed the game last evening, as well, but I could tell I wasn't giving my little girl everything she needed in life. Lisa wanted for nothing material, and Lisa loved pre-school and the daycare center. The problem was me. Or should I say Lisa and me. No, I was the problem. At home, it was only the two of us. At age four and not having reached that age with a mother at home, Lisa didn't realize what was missing – until last evening. I felt guilty that Lisa's world was without a mother figure. Lisa often ventured over to Sarah last evening and now I'd finally realized a mother figure was needed. Easier said than done.

At bedtime, Lisa cared not for a princess story, or any story. No. It was all about Danny and Sarah. Lisa was impressed and I knew questions would be forthcoming.

"Daddy, does Danny have a dad?" Lisa implored me, looking directly into my eyes. I sighed as I sat down on the bed.

"Danny's dad is gone, Lisa, and he won't be coming back." I could tell Lisa wasn't having any of this. Nope, the inquiries from my little drill sergeant continued.

"Why, Daddy?" voiced Lisa in a whisper, while she hugged her favorite teddy bear. "Why? Danny should have a daddy."

Taking a slow breath, I answered her. "Danny's dad is far away, he won't be back, and we should stop talking about why this is the way it is. Danny could get hurt feelings, and we don't want that, right, Sweetheart?" I'd hoped for no more questions. Lisa stared at the ceiling with unshed tears. My heart was breaking. Oh, my baby girl. My little girl was hurt.

"Daddy, do you like Sarah?" Lisa barely whispered as tears spilled forth.

Wiping away the tears and wrapping Lisa in my arms, I told the story of how I knew Sarah from when we went to school, that we were always friends, and we worked together at the medical center. As Lisa pondered my reply, sleepy eyes showed up and I tucked my daughter in bed for the night.

The women who chased me were out. I cared not for leaving Lisa at home while I went to a bar. Physician meetings and trips were purely for medical reasons. What a conundrum! Lisa needed a mother figure in life, and I was determined to not go down the aisle a third time.

Reflecting on last evening, I thought of Sarah. I'm sure Lisa loved Sarah already… wait…what? Loved? How did that word sneak in? Shocked, I went over last evening again. Lisa needed someone like Sarah, that was evident, indeed. Finding this 'mystery' woman was not on my horizon. Not only did Lisa need a mother figure in life, but I needed a woman to love. Wait…that word, again?

Failing at marriage in the past, I decided I could make marriage work for me, with the right woman. What was that saying? Good things come in threes. Maybe my third marriage would be the charm. It was already November, and the holidays were approaching fast, so I had no time to worry about dating until the New Year. Once life slowed down again, I'd put myself out there and try to find the right woman for both me and Lisa.

Chapter Eight

Danny

My school days were split between my teacher, Miss Gale, and a special teacher to help with my reading. A few kids made fun of me and called me names like 'stupid' and 'retard,' and they teased me for being in first grade a second time. Making fun of other kids is wrong. My teacher asked the bullies to stop, and so did my principal.

What I hated was repeating first grade! My classmates were now a year ahead of me. Why did I have to repeat first grade? I didn't understand, and the other kids made fun of me. Corey Jones got to go to transitions class first, and then to second grade, and I should be in that class. I know my head thought of Simon, a lot, and it was hard to concentrate, but Mom thought it best that I repeat first grade like my teacher wanted me to do. Still, I liked my teacher and my friends, and I had the same teacher as last year. She was awesome!

Mom asked me every day how school went and did I play with friends. I loved Miss Gale, and my reading teacher—she helped me understand what I read, and I started reading more books. I liked books! I loved learning math and drawing best. I still had two best friends from my first year of first grade and a few new ones this year.

Then Mom would ask me what I didn't like about my day at school. I'd tell Mom if I had been bullied and picked on. Mom listened carefully and helped me feel better afterwards. Mom told me how smart I was, and how fantastic I was doing in math and all the books I checked out at the school library. I liked reading, and Mom always explained any part of a book I wasn't sure of. I really liked that my mom cared about me. Sometimes, Mom called the school the next day and notified them of bad bullies the day before. My mom was my hero. Mom was here for me 100 %! A couple of the kids had no mom and I sometimes talked with them, and they missed having a real mom.

At my scout meeting tonight, the den master said a Pinewood Derby was coming up! Then I learned what the Pinewood Derby was. A Pinewood Derby is for Cub and Boy Scouts and no one else. The scouts build a derby car, and they race the cars down a sloped track, two cars at a time until the winners were chosen. The faster cars raced more times.

My den master handed out boxes to each of us, told us to take them home, and work on reading how to build the wooden race car. He said Mom could help me build it. I was excited!

At home, I showed my mom the box and we opened it on the kitchen table. Wow! This was going to be hard! I had one wooden block with plastic wheels and metal axles. Mom read to me the directions on the paper with the kit. We knew we couldn't saw the wood into a car design because we had no tools.

A thought struck me, and I shouted in excitement. "Mom, I want Dr. Aaron to help me! Dr. Aaron knows everything. Please, can we call Dr. Aaron?" Smiling at me, Mom agreed.

Mom called Dr. Aaron and when he answered, Mom explained the situation. Dr. Aaron said he could help on Thursday afternoon as he was off work that day. So, it was arranged, and I was happy.

Dr. Aaron arrived on Thursday afternoon as promised, and he brought Lisa along. He had a huge toolbox! Mom had our heated garage set up for building my derby car. We all sat together at our worktable. Mom brought out hot chocolate for us to drink and we kept our drinks on the shelf near the table. I wanted no hot chocolate on my car!

I was excited, my mom was happy, Lisa played with a doll, and Dr. Aaron laid some tools on the table. I laid out the Pinewood Derby car kit. Not a lot of car parts on the table, but Pinewood Derby cars are complicated.

"Okay, Danny, let's get started. Take a piece of paper and a pencil and draw the shape you want for your car," he instructed me. "I will draw an example on my piece of paper."

I watched as Dr. Aaron drew a car shape on his paper like the one shown on the directions in the kit, and I decided to try and make one of my own. I carefully drew an Indy racecar design, like the ones on television, and I erased a lot before I was done. "See, Dr. Aaron? I drew one! Mom, come take a look!" I shouted in excitement.

"Danny, lower your voice. Please don't shout. You are excited, but you don't need to be loud," Mom said while studying my design. "And I love the shape, Danny." Mom smiled at me and handed my design over to Dr. Aaron.

Dr. Aaron said, "Nice job, Danny. Your drawing is excellent. Next we will cut out the paper Indy car design and then trace around it on the small block of pine wood." Mom cut my paper car out evenly, and Dr. Aaron drew on the wood with a pencil around the shape I'd created. Lisa was showing my mom a new doll and doll dress. Lisa had stopped looking at what we were doing. Girls.

"Okay, everybody, stand back and I will cut the wood," said Dr. Aaron with a smile. Dr. Aaron had brought a small band saw along and my mom plugged it in on the side of the garage. Then he cut out the shape of my car. Lisa watched the action. I liked working on this car with Dr. Aaron. My dad never did anything with me, ever. Dr. Aaron was a nice guy. I wanted a real dad, one like Dr. Aaron. Lisa doesn't have a mom. I looked down at my hands and thought about things—mom and dad kinds of things.

Mom noticed I was quiet, so she insisted it was

time for a break and passed around more hot chocolate. "A Pinewood Derby car can't be completed in one night, Danny. Break time for all."

We laughed, drank our cocoa, and ate sugar cookies Mom had baked. Yummy. "Thank you, Mom."

"You are welcome, Danny. Lisa, be careful with your cup, the cocoa is hot." Mom told Lisa and me. Dr. Aaron smiled my way and I think I saw sparkles in his brown eyes.

"Now, Danny, it is time to use sandpaper and smooth this car down," Dr. Aaron said before showing me how to do it.

I sanded the soft pine wood and when I had finished, I handed my car to Dr. Aaron for inspection. Nervously, I waited to hear how I did.

"Great job, Danny! You rock! High five!" Dr Aaron reached into the toolbox and brought out glass paint bottles. "Look these colors over and decide the color you want your car to be."

Dr. Aaron explained how the tires and axles slide in on my car, and he showed my mom and me. Then we talked about how much my car should weigh. Dr. Aaron said my derby car could not weigh over five ounces and asked my mom to get the small kitchen weigh scale. My car weighed 2.5 ounces. Bigger cars weigh more but I made mine the shape of an Indy racecar so mine weighed less.

"This is soft wood, Danny. That means additional weight must be added."

"How do I do that? Can we do that?" I questioned.

"Let me grab a few light weights from my toolbox and we can see what will work the best, Danny."

After getting three flat metal weights, Dr. Aaron placed one weight on the scale. My car weighed 3.6 ounces—not enough! Dr. Aaron removed the weight and placed a second one on the scale. The combined weight of my cut-out car shape of wood, the plastic wheels, metal axles that looked like four nails to me, and the weight on the scale came in just under the maximum allowed, at 4.8 ounces. Yay!

"When can I paint it, Dr. Aaron?" I was excited and jumping up and down. I wanted my car to be bright yellow.

"Not yet, Danny."

Using a special knife, Dr. Aaron carefully carved out a small area underneath my car. Then I added a special glue inside the carved part and Dr. Aaron placed the weight inside. "No more can be done now, Danny, until the glue hardens, and the weight is secured."

"What?" I asked with my eyes huge. "When do I get to paint it?"

"Tomorrow, Danny. I will leave the yellow paint and a paint brush here. Come help me pack up my tools, please. Lisa is sleepy so we need to go home now."

"Okay! Thank you, Dr. Aaron," I said as I grabbed his legs and hugged them.

Dr. Aaron and Lisa left, and I took a bath and went to bed with a smile on my face and ready for happy dreams.

Chapter Nine

Sarah

Grandma Cordie.... I need you. Please visit me in my dreams tonight. I'm confused, Danny needs a father figure, Lisa needs a mom, and I'm lonely. I need a husband, but I swore off men. Please bring your Cherokee wisdom to me tonight. I'm afraid to trust a man, any man, even my friend, Aaron, yet he is different and so easy on the eyes. I do trust Aaron; I don't trust me. I know he won't like my body. I'm scared, and Cordie? Two little hearts are involved. Nudge me to make the right decisions for Danny's sake.

Aaron had been super kind yesterday. Danny and Aaron worked together intently with Danny listening to everything seriously. My son was excited, but he had been fully engrossed in the car making business last evening.

Danny's excitement continued this morning, running into the kitchen as I cooked. "Settle down, sweetheart, and eat your breakfast. You asked for blueberry pancakes, and this is your plate!" After pouring myself a cup of black coffee, I sat down at the table with Danny. "Since it's Saturday, what do you want to do today?"

"I want to paint my derby car, Mom. Can you show me the right way and then watch me paint? Please?' Danny jumped up and down.

"Sure, Danny. We can do it after breakfast, but chores are done first, okay?" I hummed as the kitchen was cleaned, and a load of laundry started.

"Okay, Danny, it's time. Thank you for helping me. Please go get the car, yellow paint, and paint brush." Danny shot off to grab the derby car and paint. I placed newspaper on the table and the car and paint were placed on top. I showed Danny how much paint to use and to spread it evenly—not too thick. Paint the bottom of the car and one side only. Then the car will dry before the rest of the paint goes on.

"Okay, Mom, I can do that," Danny responded happily.

The grin Danny wore while he painted the car warmed my heart. Placing Danny in Boy Scouts was the right thing to do. All things scouting was his shining element. As Danny happily painted the derby car, I baked a chocolate cake for dessert tonight. Of all things, Danny didn't know I baked his favorite cake. That was a first!

Danny has been happier and more animated. My son was almost back to normal, meaning before Simon's illness and death, and my divorce. As a matter of fact, Danny was the happiest ever in his life. My heart soared high above the clouds. Now to keep my little boy in this happy place.

With a deep sigh, I pondered my situation. I truly can't ask Aaron to be there every time Danny asked to call. How could I? It just wouldn't be fair to Aaron or Lisa. Lisa needed a family, and she had a daddy only at home—a family of two. My good friend Aaron had been kind and took to my son instantly, but it was wrong to monopolize the time he could spend with Lisa. Aaron had relatives down in Colorado Springs, but they were busy, too. I figured all would get together come Thanksgiving, in two weeks.

As a busy doctor, Aaron worked trauma, which meant regular shifts. Unlike surgeons and other doctors, Aaron wasn't called to the floor or a unit, and 'on call' status was rare. The next time we worked, I hoped Aaron would broach this subject first. Call me timid… no one would believe that if I was watched in the ER, competent and steady as a nurse. Hesitant as a woman? Oh yes, that was me. Did true love exist? Only in fairytales.

In the afternoon, I took Danny to watch a movie playing at the theater in Bel Mar, a nearby neighborhood in Lakewood. Danny chose a Disney movie, *Toy Story 4*. After purchasing popcorn and sodas, we found seats in the theater. Danny was smiling and animated before the movie started. My son had changed. The last time we tried to see a movie on the silver screen, Danny cried as he was still heartbroken over the loss of his brother. This time, he watched it without crying or being sad.

Scouting was a great influence on my son, and so was Aaron. Decisions. What do I do? I didn't want my friendship with Aaron to be damaged, yet I kept coming back to that gorgeous hunk of a man in my visions, all lean and muscular. He was an Adonis, and I was struck dumb by suddenly realizing I had loved Aaron since high school. I thought it had been infatuation, but now I knew differently. My poor muddled brain. Decisions. It had always been Danny and me, and now I had to make the right decisions for both of us.

During supper, Danny and I chatted about the movie and then I dished up his favorite cake, chocolate.

"Mom, please check my derby car and tell me if its dry." Danny was brimming with a happiness I'd never seen last a full day in the past.

"After chores are done, Danny. I want the dishes cleaned up, and the laundry taken to your room, and placed in the drawers and closet. No dumping on the floor, young man." Danny obliged me, and after chores were done, I checked on the derby car. It was dry, so I placed fresh newsprint on the kitchen table.

When Danny saw the newsprint, he clapped both hands and went to get the car and paint. I instructed Danny on how to place the car on the top of a small cup, so he could paint the top and the other side of his car, and do any touch ups, if needed. Talk about pure joy, it bubbled out of Danny like a waterfall, as I sat and watched the car turn completely yellow.

When done, the car was left to dry, and Danny took a bath. My son was tired and winding down, so I gave a kiss to both cheeks as Danny fell asleep. I went to bed early, after my shower, and prayed I would dream of the right answers for Danny and me.

Chapter Ten

Aaron

After tucking Lisa in last night, I replayed in my mind the events at Sarah's apartment, working together on Danny's derby car. It was wonderful spending time with Sarah and Danny yesterday. Danny is so special to me. He truly is a precious and remarkable child. The four of us meshed in a perfect click.

Sarah smiled more during that short time frame than I'd seen since high school. My heart ripped apart when I thought of Sarah never actually laughing at work. My good friend hurt, and I didn't even notice! Sarah was always professional and courteous at work. You wouldn't know how much pain she carried inside by watching her work, but I should have seen it. I failed my friend, and I hung my head in shame. I'd been a dreadful friend to Sarah. I hung my head in shame. How could I fix this?

Sarah and Danny have needs just like Lisa and I

have needs. The four of us were fantastic together yesterday! Yes, but now what? Sarah is enclosed inside a hard shell. I must reach through and help my friend. I decided then and there to make time to be with Sarah and Danny each week. Since Lisa would be with us, both children would benefit, and I might be able to help Sarah. I wonder…no …yes… Sarah would make a perfect mother for Lisa. Where did that thought come from? I wished Danny was my son. What? Why did I think that? Wow. I don't know about that. I have a wonderful friend in Sarah. Would this complicate our relationship? No. Was I falling in love with my treasured Sarah? I am! Indeed, all points flowed back towards Sarah. One problem: Sarah refused to marry again. I knew this because another ER nurse, Suzy Hill, informed me of this right after Sarah was divorced. Heck! Have Sarah and Danny healed from the abuse? Could I reach them? I must try.

I'd tread the murky waters lightly and carefully. With that in mind, I'd ring Sarah up in the morning. This called for baby steps. I'd invite Sarah and Danny out for coffee and hot chocolate tomorrow afternoon. All four of us could meet at Carriage Crossing for refreshments and the kids could check out the bookstore area of the coffeeshop. Carriage

Crossing was a family friendly business and perfect for a get-together. With this in my head, I fell asleep.

I waited until I knew Sarah and Danny would be home from church before I called. Sarah picked up on the second ring.

"Good morning, Sarah. Have I caught you at a good time?"

"You have great timing, Aaron. We just got home from church and Danny is eating a roast beef sandwich. What's up?

"Well, if you're not busy later, would you and Danny like to meet up around 2p.m. at Carriage Crossing? Lisa has been begging me to see Danny again." Hopefully, Sarah would say yes.

"Could Danny and I have a raincheck on that? Let's get together at my place instead. How does that sound? I'll have refreshments for all, and Danny wants to make sure the wheels and axles are placed on the derby car correctly, and, well, Danny wants Dr. Aaron to supervise."

Laughing into my mobile, I responded, "Sure, Sarah. We can be there around 2 p.m. I'm happy to help Danny anytime."

"Okay, Aaron. Sounds like a plan to me. Until later, then. Goodbye."

Chapter Eleven

Sarah

Snow was softly falling when Aaron and Lisa

arrived in a black, shiny, Jeep Grand Cherokee Limited 4 x 4, a couple of years newer than my own. I smiled as I thought about our choice of vehicle. I remembered that Aaron had a Jeep Wrangler in high school. Funny how the mind works on matters that seem trivial, yet maybe not? Was this a sign?

Grandma Cordie, is this the sign? We both love Jeeps. Surely, I need a stronger sign than this? Aaron is my best friend. I don't want to lose that friendship, ever! Help me, Cordie, please. I'm so confused and utterly unsure of myself. No man would want a damaged woman, and I don't have the kind of body men crave; particularly a female without a perfectly sculpted figure eight body.

I opened the door as Aaron rang the bell. After showing where to leave coats and boots, I helped Lisa take her wet snowy boots off, both went into the living room, and warmed up by the fire burning in the river rock stone fireplace. Danny squealed with sheer delight upon seeing Aaron and Lisa.

"Mom, I must show Dr. Aaron and Lisa my room." Danny spoke and I nodded my head as the children took off.

Leading the way, Danny swaggered just a little bit before arriving at the door. Inside, my son's room had walls of soft blue and framed posters of his favorite live events we'd attended, such as Sesame Street Live and other children's events, plus posters of Danny's favorite football and baseball players, and one acrylic painting of Simon, a head portrait, near the desk.

Above the bed hung a lovely wooden crucifix with a silver Jesus. To the right of that hung a large guardian angel I had cross-stitched just so Danny would be surrounded by angels on all sides. Danny's bed sported Disney *Car* sheets and comforter. Lisa was impressed, her eyes huge.

"Wow, Danny. You have lots of cars and Ninja Turtles! Can we play?" Peering up at me, I gave a smile and said yes. Both children's eyes were literally sparkling. A moment to treasure forever.

"Go ahead and play for a bit; I will finish up

refreshments in the kitchen." I smiled at both children and all the way into the kitchen.

When I turned around to place a plate of chocolate chip cookies on the table, I caught Aaron staring at me. Those deep dark eyes bored into me, and I was nervous.

"You're gorgeous, Sarah. Sorry to be forward, but I can't help it. You're the epitome of the ideal woman and you're great with children," Aaron stated while he continued to stare, and my mouth hung open.

I was rather shocked, I didn't expect to hear those words coming from Aaron, at all, and this was new territory for me. No one ever called me gorgeous in the past. Ideal woman? No way. Great with children? I agreed with that.

Finally, I replied, "Thank you, Aaron, for the wonderful compliment." I turned back to the coffee as my cheeks flamed a bright red. What does Aaron see that I don't? Wait. Great with kids. Maybe Aaron wanted a mother for Lisa, and I was a safe bet since we were such great friends for a very long time? Confused I silently spoke with Grandma Cordie.

Grandma Cordie, I'm confused. Aaron just shattered my brain with compliments and spoke of how good I am with children. But Aaron doesn't love me. Why did that pop into my head? Please point the way, Cordie. Guide me. Give me your wise Cherokee thoughts. I love you.

With a smile plastered on my face, I turned around with a tray of coffee and hot chocolate, as I called out, "Danny and Lisa, please come to the kitchen, snacks are ready."

Both children were animated and chattered between bites, as we sipped drinks and ate cookies. I smiled as I watched how the children reacted and then looked over towards Aaron and smiled. He smiled back.

After eating snacks, Danny spoke up, "Dr. Aaron, can you help with my derby car, please?

"Sure, Danny. No problem," Aaron replied. "First, help me clean up the table."

"No, Aaron. Danny will help me clean the table and place dishes in the dishwasher. You two are guests. Five minutes, okay?" I smiled back and found myself lost in those dark brown smoldering eyes.

After placing one sheet of newsprint on the kitchen table, Danny brought out the yellow derby car, axles and plastic wheels and placed them on the table.

"Danny, great paint job!" Dr. Aaron exclaimed as he smiled at my son. Danny beamed with pride.

"Thank you," Danny answered happily as he asked Aaron how to add the tires to the car.

"Okay, then, let us take a look." Aaron looked at the wheels, axles, and the instruction sheet. Then he placed one axle through one wheel and slid it by hand into the grooved slot. After spinning the wheel, Aaron pushed it in a bit further. The wheel was able to spin, then he showed Danny how close the wheel was to the car. Aaron placed the last three wheels on the racecar and explained to Danny that if they were too close to the car, the wheels wouldn't move correctly, yet they had to be close. Reaching into his pocket, Aaron brought out a tube of graphite.

"This is graphite, Danny, and a little bit goes a long way. Graphite will help your wheels move easier and smoother." Then he handed the racecar to my son with graphite on the wheels. Danny pushed the car forward on the table and it went straight ahead.

"Awesome, Dr. Aaron! Yay! Can we decorate my car like the Indy cars on television, Mom?" Aaron brought out a sheet of sticky back decals and between them, decals were added. The car truly looked like an Indy racecar.

"Thank you…," Danny sang out happily. "Dr. Aaron, would you and Lisa come and watch me race my car this Saturday at the Scout cabin?"

"Sure, Danny, what time?"

Danny said the races start at 2 p.m., and I gave Aaron directions to the Scout cabin.

Lisa was sleepy and Aaron made goodbyes and thanked Danny and me for the snacks. We all would sleep great tonight. What a perfect day.

Chapter Twelve

Danny

Wow, I thought. Dr. Aaron helped me with my racecar and I'm not even his son. He's not my dad. I wish he was my dad. Lisa could be my little sister! I hope we can get together soon. Dr Aaron did say he and Lisa would come to the Pinewood Derby on Saturday. What should I do if the other boys think he's my dad? What would Mom say? I guess I'll know on Saturday. I got ready for school and ate my breakfast with Mom.

The day of the Pinewood Derby arrived! I can't wait for Dr. Aaron to see my genius idea. Mom and I had carefully weighed my racecar on the scale. I wanted to add a plastic windshield, steering wheel, and half of a Lego man on my car to make it look like a real

Indy car! My car weighed out okay, so we carefully glued the pieces in place last night. I'm excited and Mom drove through the snowy streets to the Scout cabin. A large fire was glowing when we walked inside. I ran over to my friends, Tommy, and Nathan, and we inspected all the cars lined up on the table. Mom placed snacks on the snacks table and sat down with other parents just as Dr. Aaron and Lisa arrived. They made it! Yay! The cars were so cool and different colors. When the scout master told us to take our seats, I sat down with Tommy and Nathan.

The meeting was called to order. We do this in scouts. Corey Jones walked down the middle of the room with the United States of America flag and all scouts stood tall and repeated the Pledge of Allegiance while doing the scout salute, a salute we did to show respect for the flag and in greeting others. Together we recited the Boy Scout oath because we always started our meetings that way. It felt like a real ceremony.

We always started scout meetings this way, a real ceremony. The den master then told all of us that he knew we were ready to race, and we were instructed in the process for today's race. The assistant scout master helped the scout master set up the racetrack.

It curved down like a roller coaster!

The den master had a clipboard with paper and brackets for the race drawn on it. My name was on the second bracket. Each scout was instructed to get their car and then to sit back down on the sidelines until their name was called. This was happening! One by one we were called for a weigh in on the racecars. No scout had too much weight so no one was eliminated!

Racing began and the first two boys got up when called and placed their cars on the two tracks. The den master pulled down a wooden lever and the cars were off and racing to the bottom of the track! The scout with the fastest car advanced to the next round and the scout with the slowest car also advanced in the lower bracket. No car was eliminated yet. My scout master explained this as double elimination.

Double elimination brackets are broken up into a winner's bracket and a loser's bracket. The winner of the loser's bracket played the winner of the winner's bracket for first place. Losers of matches in the winner's bracket would then drop down one spot and play another loser to see who advanced in the loser's bracket. This meant that each car raced more than once!

My car raced second and won in the winner's round! I looked up at Dr. Aaron, and he smiled and clapped his hands. Mom smiled at me, and Lisa played with a doll. Girls! What do girls know about cars anyway!

I won my second race, too! One car was fast as lightning, it was Davy's, and the car was shaped like a rocket! Davy painted his car gold with red stripes. I never thought of stripes. I bet Davy worked hard on getting that rocket shape sanded. It looked like a half rocket laid on its side with the wheel's underneath.

At the end of the Pinewood Derby, results were announced. I won second place, and I received an awesome huge trophy. Mom was taking pictures like crazy—she always took lots of pictures. First, second and third place winners stood next to each other for official photos for the newspaper. The den master announced the *Best of Show* winner. I won! This trophy was bigger, and the judges liked my car the best – I think they liked the shape, the decals, and racecar driver I'd placed on it like a real Indy car. The scouts who didn't place in the race received a 'Participant Trophy.'.

Afterwards, we all had snacks and drinks, and then the scouts got together in a 'Troop Circle' followed by the closing flag ceremony.

Dr. Aaron helped me carry one trophy as I couldn't carry both trophies and my racecar. That was nice. Dr. Aaron congratulated me again and told me how smart I was to come up with the driver on my car. We said our goodbyes and I thanked Dr. Aaron and Lisa for coming.

Chapter Thirteen

Aaron

Danny was thrilled at the Pinewood Derby yesterday. The pure joy on that little face warmed my heart. Sarah smiled often and I swear a glow emanated from that perfect face. The four of us made the ideal team. Is that enough to base a marriage on? Lisa was fast asleep, and I sipped on Crown and Coke as I thought over all the positives and negatives.

My history of two failed marriages were my negatives as far as I could tell. Sarah had been hurt a lot, and in ways I didn't know. Could I turn those negatives into positives? Could I get Sarah to open up to me?

On the positive side, the four of us meshed perfectly. Sarah and I shared the best of friendships and a belief in a shared Catholic faith. A friendship was definitely a strong base for taking a relationship to the next level, set in stone, in a manner of speaking.

Sarah wasn't out for a 'meal ticket' or for what I could provide materially speaking, or the status of wife to a physician. Kind, level-headed, smart, Sarah was rather gorgeous. As in WOW gorgeous. Blond waves of hair spilling over her shoulders, those cobalt blue eyes, her rear end a perfect heart shape in tight jeans, her breasts looked perky (well, she had a bra on) under that T-shirt… I must be losing it to think these thoughts… No, I'm smitten, and I've begun to realize how bad I have it for Sarah. I honestly love Sarah! *I love Sarah.* Could I get Sarah to open her heart and allow my love inside?

The four of us needed to get together again, soon. I recalled seeing a poster in the physicians' lounge about horse drawn hay wagon rides and a straw bale maze. I decided to invite Sarah and Danny.

Halfway through today's shift I caught Sarah alone, writing in a patient chart. "Sarah, would you and Danny be interested in going to the Scarecrow Farm with Lisa and me? I read about the wagon rides and a straw bale maze."

"Great minds think alike, Aaron. I was planning on taking Danny this Saturday. Would that day work out? I thought to arrive around 3 p.m."

Anything would work out with you, Sarah. "That

sounds like a perfect time for the kids to have fun right before Thanksgiving," I concurred. "How about I pick the two of you up?"

Sarah nodded yes just as a patient call light came on. She went behind the nurse's desk to answer it. What a cute behind Sarah had, still heart shaped in the scrub pants. Why did I not notice that before?

The snow fell lightly as I pulled up to Sarah's apartment, and Danny and Sarah came on out to my Jeep. After getting in and securing seatbelts, I drove towards Scarecrow Farm, about a 20-minute drive.

When we pulled in and parked, the kids wanted to try the straw bale maze first. I donated money for the four of us and off we went, the kids running ahead. The bales were huge, and I couldn't see over them, and I was tall! Danny led us with Lisa closing in until my daughter stumbled to the ground, fell, and scraped a knee.

Sarah was faster than me and reached Lisa first. I was astonished to see Sarah holding Lisa and soothing her. I was completely astounded when

Sarah brought out a small first aid kit from a bag and cleaned Lisa's wound, applied antibiotic cream, and covered the abrasion with a Band-Aid. Sarah was prepared for little incidents. I was not and I'm a doctor? *What the heck?*

"I love how prepared you are, Sarah. Thank you for taking care of Lisa's knee." I knelt upon the straw covered path and checked for other abrasions.

"No problem, Aaron, I always carry a small first aid kit in my bag, and I have a full-size larger kit in the back of my Jeep. In nursing, I was taught to be prepared and the boy scouts are taught to be prepared." Winking at me, Sarah admonished me in mock, "Aren't doctors prepared?" Then Sarah laughed out loud. Seeing this was pure delight for me, I wanted to see that look on Sarah's face all the time.

"You got me, Sarah. I do have my packed doctor's bag in my Jeep, too, but no small portable first aid kit in my bag. I don't carry a purse like you do. Does that mean I'm still prepared?" I quizzed back with a laugh.

Before Sarah could reply, Danny had run up to see what had happened and he told Lisa that his mom fixed the "boo-boo" just like when he scraped a knee or elbow. "I like my mom being a nurse!" Danny smiled broadly.

Lisa had stopped crying and told Danny, "I like my daddy being a doctor! Can we finish the straw bale maze, Daddy?"

"Sure, let's get going." I smiled down at the kids' eager faces. Off we went and we did get turned around a couple of times, yet victorious in the end.

Outside the maze, we decided to buy warm apple cider to drink as we waited in line for our turn at a hay rack ride. The horse drawn hay wagon came around and we climbed on. Well, Danny climbed up fast, Sarah followed, and I handed Lisa up and climbed in after. The children were warm and animated, talking about the horse. Sarah shivered from the chill in the November air, and I placed my arm around those slim shoulders. Sarah froze for a second, then allowed me to keep my arm in place.

When our ride was over, I helped Lisa and Sarah down as Danny climbed down without assistance. It was time to leave and at the gate, both children chose a free miniature pumpkin to take home. I dropped off Sarah and Danny at the apartment, and both smiled and said thanks. As the door closed, I felt bereft. Bereft of what? I was deprived of Sarah and

Danny. I had this love thing badly. Danny needs a dad, Lisa needs a mom, but I need Sarah and Sarah needs me. I knew my love wouldn't waver, but how to convince Sarah?

Chapter Fourteen

Sarah

Danny and I enjoyed a wonderful time at Scarecrow Farm. Both children had a great time, and Danny wasn't sad at all. Aaron and Lisa are good for Danny. When Aaron placed one arm around me during the hay rack ride, I froze for a second before I melted into the warm reassurance of what? My stomach fluttered with that single touch. *What?* Am I falling in love with Aaron? Does Aaron truly love me? When Aaron had placed one arm around my shoulders, I'd turned my face away, I didn't want to betray my innermost feelings and heartache. Danny obviously loves Aaron and Lisa. I'm the hold up. Aaron hasn't seen me. I mean, he hasn't seen my body. He hasn't seen my ugly, irregular, and scarred body. The body my ex had been disgusted with. Yet Aaron isn't like my ex. Aaron was sexy, with a side of charm, and a heaping dose of charisma.

Grandma Cordie. My body, a figure eight hourglass shape it is not. I'm so insecure about my body. Could I really let Aaron see it? I need you, Grandma. I'm confused and lost. I need your Cherokee wisdom. Mostly, I'm scared, this is new territory for me and I've nothing to judge my honest feelings against, nothing to compare what I feel now with anything in my past. I love Aaron. Are my feelings real? I realize I never loved my ex. I knew not what real love felt like. Are my hopes and dreams real, have I missed a key piece of evidence? Please come to me, Cordie.

I needed to pray to the Lord. He would help me and guide me in the way I was to travel.

Jesus, help me make the right decisions - ones that won't be detrimental to my son or me. Aaron is such a funny and kind man with eyes I melt inside of, expressive and deep. I have an ache, deep inside me, for an enduring and all-encompassing love with Aaron. I'm afraid of my hopes and dreams shattering into millions of slivers, each sliver slicing into Danny and me. I pray for direction in this relationship for it is a relationship with four hearts involved, two of them little hearts. I pray You guide me in the right direction and the right decisions. Amen.

Thanksgiving was four days away and I still had some shopping to do for Danny and me. It would be our second Thanksgiving without Simon and only the two of us, again. I had a small turkey, but I needed to buy fresh fruit and veggies after work today. Keeping that mental list in my head, I ran to the ambulance bay as two motor vehicle accident victims arrived, having driven off Clear Creek Canyon Road and into the frozen waters of Clear Creek. This couple was lucky. They only suffered bone fractures but were both alert and oriented. My friend, Suzy Hill, RN and another doctor, Dr. Michael Jones, took over the care for this couple.

Memories flooded back invading my mind… no one wants you… you want it in the rear… my ex sneered at me… yes, I will have you no matter if you did have Danny three days ago… the rape… all the rapes… remember, you are mine only, you can't leave with Danny… you made your bed with me, you lay in it… until he finally passed out. The memories of the fateful night when Danny was injured at the hands of my ex, his bruised body and swollen face rushed at me.

Aaron brought me out of my reverie asking a question. "I'm sorry, Aaron, I lost my train of thought. What did you need?"

"Are you okay, Sarah? You looked a million miles away." Aaron looked concerned.

"I'm fine, truly. I was thinking about the holidays is all. What was it you needed?"

"Sarah, I invited you and Danny to my home for Thanksgiving. Unless you have other plans? My mother and sister are coming up from Colorado Springs like each year, and it would be lovely if you and Danny were present. My home has plenty of room. Please say yes, Lisa wants you and Danny to come."

I dropped the chart I'd been working on, and Aaron knelt next to me and helped me gather papers. Our fingers touched and I felt like I'd been scorched, I tingled all the way down to my toes. Did Aaron feel it, too? I looked up, my gaze transfixed, and then I came back to my senses. "Thank you, Aaron. And thank you for the invitation. Danny will love doing Thanksgiving together. What time?"

"Will 11 a.m. work out?" Aaron inquired.

"Absolutely," I replied as I placed the chart on top of a stack. "Shall I bring a few side dishes?

"Sure, Sarah. My mom and sister always make enough for a lot of leftovers, but, please, bring some of the favorites that you and Danny like." Aaron smiled as he walked away, Thanksgiving now settled, as I gazed at that man's backside going down the hall.

Chapter Fifteen

Aaron

My family always gathered at my large eight-bedroom timbered and river rock stone home on Lookout Mountain for Thanksgiving. I particularly loved my river rock stone fireplace as it gave off perfect vibes of warmth and friendliness. Looking out my front windows, I watched my homes' lights reflect off the small lake on my property. My home included four bedrooms with private baths, and my mom and sister each took one of those.

Of course, I had the main master bedroom, the adjoining bath with double sinks, two-person shower, a jacuzzi, and two huge walk-in closets. My room was decorated in a classic 1980s-era theme and featured an elevated fireplace surrounded by backlit smoky quartz. Muted shades of sand and light brown colored bedding completed my king size matching wooden bed.

Lisa had the last of the suites, decorated with a custom-made Charles H. Beckley bed upholstered in Butterfly by Lori Weitzner for Sahco Hesslein. A playful vibe imbued the pink and purple color scheme that matched Lisa's favorite colors. I did spoil my daughter, but I could, so I did. Lisa never received everything she asked for, but I gave the 'mains' and then some. The other four bedrooms received occasional use by friends who came to stay for a brief getaway from life in the city.

My mom, Alice, lived with my sister, Cindy Anderson Woods, in a well-appointed three-bedroom condo down in Colorado Springs. Alice was 40 when I was born, so now at 73, she's not as active as in the past. Widowed for 20 years, Mom refused to take off the wedding rings, David, my dad had designed. My parents' marriage brought forth one son, me, and one daughter, my sister Cindy. With the passing of Cindy's husband, Cindy had been left childless. Together, they ran a coffeeshop in "Springs" named Docs Coffee.

Soon, both would gather in my home for Thanksgiving. My housekeeper, Sadie Edwards, had already freshened up the guest rooms for my guests. Sadie was a dream of a housekeeper. Sadie always made dinner for Lisa and me, kept in the refrigerator ready to reheat upon our arrival home. This worked out perfectly as I never knew if I would leave the hospital on time. Sadie lived in a small two-bedroom timbered guesthouse less than 100 yards from my back door. Sadie had never married and had no living family. I found a true gem in Sadie, and Sadie found useful work, a home, nice salary, and family with Lisa and me. Every year Sadie prepared the turkey and trimmings. At 55, she was raring to keep all traditions going.

Since we went to school together, my mom and sister knew Sarah and Danny, and they both knew about the huge loss when Simon passed, and Sarah's divorce.

Sadie was busy in the kitchen, and the scent of Thanksgiving turkey filled the air. Guests would be arriving in short order.

My mom and Cindy arrived first. Mom looked well and dressed in a Christmas sweater, blue jeans, and hiking boots—the boots to traverse the snow in a safer manner. Cindy wore blue jeans and boots as well, and an emerald, green silk blouse that matched the eyes which twinkled up at me. After hugs and kisses, the boots left in the foyer on a rug, coats and scarfs hung to dry, we headed for the fireplace to warm up after the chill of the outdoors. The side dishes were taken to the kitchen by Sadie and me.

Sarah and Danny arrived 30 minutes later. My sister and mom were kind and visited with Sarah and Danny as they recalled times of old high school memories, and more.

Danny and Lisa played happily by the fireplace. What could possibly make this Thanksgiving better?

Sadie called out that the meal was ready, so we all went into the dining room as Sarah and Cindy helped bring the side dishes to the table. Last year there was five of us, this year seven. I liked this year better. I said grace and thanks in prayer for all our collective blessings.

"Dr. Aaron, I'm hungry. Can't you carve that turkey now? I want a leg!" Danny asked. Everyone laughed and I carved a slice for Danny first as Sarah helped serve both children side dishes. As I glanced across the table, I noted Cindy looked sullen, and directly at Sarah. Was Cindy not well or possibly jealous?

After our meal ended, the kids cleaned up and sat on a rug near the fire, with Danny reading a book to Lisa. Mom, Sarah, Cindy, and I helped Sadie clear the table and clean the dining room and kitchen with dishes in the dishwasher or already dried and put away.

Contented and lost in my thoughts, Cindy had to ask me twice if we could talk in the hall, privately.

"What's on your mind, Cindy? You didn't seem to be feeling well at dinner. Do I need to know something?"

"Well, Aaron, it's Sarah. Why on earth did you invite Sarah and Danny to our family dinner? Sarah served the sides to Lisa! Have you lost your mind?"

Confused and puzzled by this outspoken diatribe of wordage spilling from Cindy's mouth, I simply gawked at her. "What do you mean? You have known Sarah and Danny for years. Why shouldn't they be included this year? I certainly have plenty of room and food."

Cindy gave me an exasperated look before stating in a louder and much angrier voice, "Sarah is a gold digger. Is that what you want? Sarah is after your money, your prestige and what you can do for Danny. Have you lost your mind, Aaron?"

I was taken aback by her words and the venom in which they were delivered. "Sarah is *not* a gold digger! You know Sarah makes a lot of money as a busy nurse working trauma. You simply don't make sense, at all, Cindy! Stop this nonsense now!" I was incensed. "Furthermore, I *love* Sarah! Did you hear that? I love Sarah, and Danny, too. You don't know the definition of true love."

Taking a deep breath, I stated, "As I've said before, I love Sarah and Danny, I even told you that I loved Sarah before I had the chance to tell Sarah myself! That fact makes me angry. Be nice. Be kind. If not, you won't be allowed back into my home!" Then I walked away, leaving Cindy steaming mad with her mouth hanging open. How dare Cindy try to ruin a beautiful day.

Unknown to me, all those present had heard the argument. Upon entering my living room no one looked at me or said a single word. Danny and Lisa sat quietly with tearful eyes, and Sarah was crying. My mom was hugging Sarah and both children closely. Great! What more could possibly happen? Mom was upset and I hated seeing what I had just walked into. What a blasted day! Things had been perfect, and now this.

After apologizing to my wonderful guests, I turned around and demanded Cindy apologize right then and there! Reluctantly, Cindy apologized to

Sarah and Danny, then to Mom and Lisa. My sister ran out of the room and up to the bedroom that had been set up for her.

Well, it was out. My only choice was to sit down and explain this to my mom, Sarah, and the kids. "I'm so sorry you overheard what Cindy said, and Sarah, my sister was wrong, very wrong. Sarah, I do love you! I also love you, Danny. Is that a problem for you, Mom?"

Mom declared with a huge smile, "Bravo Aaron! You've done well and picked a winner this time. Sarah is perfect! A perfect match for you. Danny adores you! I'll speak to Cindy later when she's calmer. For now, I want to stay here and give comfort and support as needed. And, Sarah, I have fallen in love with you and Danny. You are both like family already, and I would be proud if you married my son someday, if that is what God wants, and the four of you want the same."

"Thanks, Mom. Sarah, I wish to speak with you, Danny, and Lisa." I cared not that my mom was in the room, Sadie quietly left for the kitchen.

"My feelings are out, I love you and Danny, and when you are ready, I want to be a family legally. I'm so sorry you heard it the way you did. When you are ready, I plan to propose."

Sarah responded, "To be honest, I love you and Lisa, too. I don't know how, or if, this will work out. Let's give Cindy some time. I'm nervous as all get out and I have many insecurities and issues to work through. I also vowed a promise to my son that nothing and no one would ever hurt us again, and now, well, Danny hurts." I cuddled Danny with Lisa at my side.

"That sounds like an adult plan and provides time for us to work problems out. The snow is quite heavy now, and not safe to drive in. Sarah, I think it would be best for you and Danny to spend the night here, the weather is frightful. You can share one bedroom together if it makes you more comfortable. I plan on asking Sadie to stay as well for safety reasons. I don't want Sadie walking in the heavy snow, and she usually stays over when the weather is bad."

Sarah agreed and later, she and Danny climbed the stairs towards their room. Danny's face had been somber the entire evening. I prayed things would work out.

Please Lord, I love Sarah and Danny. I can't lose them. Guide me with Your glory. Amen.

Chapter Sixteen

Sarah

Back in my apartment the next day, Danny and I talked about yesterday. My son was a little bit sad, and he asked me what 'gold digger' meant, as he ate breakfast. "Danny, a 'gold digger' is a woman who dates a man for the money he has, the wealth, the fancy houses, and the status that can be obtained. I'm sure Cindy didn't mean the words 'gold digger and we simply surprised everyone.

"Mom, you are not a 'gold digger'! You work hard! "You take good care of me, make sure I have food and am never hungry, take me to do fun things, you drive a nice, warm car, and pay for us to live here. Cindy was wrong." Danny stated in a matter-of-fact manner.

"Remember the way you felt, Danny, when you were not sure of something? That is how Cindy felt. You and me with Aaron and Lisa surprised everyone yesterday. I'd not known that Aaron hadn't told his mom and sister we were invited. Aaron's mother loves you dearly. Cindy liked you, too. Do you understand, sweetheart?"

Danny nodded yes. "I think I understand. I love Dr. Aaron and Lisa, too. Mom, could we be a true family? A *real* family? Would you marry Aaron and then I'd have a *real* dad? Lisa would be my *real* sister!" Danny grinned, and he enunciated the word real in no uncertain terms. Only Danny would do that, and he brought a smile to my face and heart.

"Are you sure, Danny? I made a promise to you, that I would protect you, that it would be the two of us only, together. I don't want to change that unless you are sure. You come first, Danny."

Danny nodded yes with huge glowing blue eyes. I smiled at my son, then asked if he was ready to decorate our Christmas tree.

The Christmas tree Danny and I decorated was truly an 'angel' tree. We hung precious angel ornaments for each Christmas that arrived since Simon went to Heaven. This year Danny and I each hung one angel, marking the second Christmas without Simon. I held Danny up so he could top the tree with a larger beautiful angel. Reverently, together we hung a paper angel with Simon's face on it, cut from a photo, that he'd made in pre-school. It was his last Christmas on earth, although we'd not had any idea at the time. Simon's angel was front and center.

Due to the issues with Cindy on Thanksgiving, I chose not to take my son to the Christmas family gathering at Aaron's home on Lookout Mountain in Golden, thus Danny and I remained at home following Christmas Eve mass at St. Mary's.

On Christmas Day, Danny awoke, and was chomping at the bit, eagerly waiting to open presents. Danny loved opening gifts and finding a real large-scale model of a Galaxy-class starship - the U.S.S. Enterprise NCC-1701-D. The star ship sat on a large pedestal and had battery operated lights. Danny was all things Star Trek: The Next Generation. My son loved Captain Jean-Luc Picard, and all things Klingon and Borg. Of course, I gave my son new clothes and boots, all the normal new attire essentials and extras for kids, and a Kansas City Chiefs coat! We lived in Bronco's territory, but it was the Chiefs for both of us!

That night, before sleep, I'd thought over the last year and a half. It had been way more than a year and a half since I'd had sex, and that was rape at the hands of my ex! That man never cared if I'd just had a baby three days prior, or my tubes tied with full incision, and against my wishes only so he could prevent me from having more babies, or anything else. He literally took what he wanted, when he wanted, whether it was me or another woman. Suddenly, I realized intimate life had never been good for me. I wondered, was this the normal for all women? I allowed my thoughts to wander around, as I searched and raced to make sense of everything, of what I'd never known.

Jesus, Help me with my crazy thoughts right now. I know that man and woman were created by God, and I know my Bible. I'm not embarrassed by my thoughts, but I need guidance on how to proceed, especially with Aaron and any possible future sexual relations. I pray in Your name, Amen

Sex. Men want it, but do most women like it? Maybe my feelings are based on what my ex did to me? The way my friend, Suzy, talks, sex is more than fun. I'm so embarrassed.

Grandma Cordie, I need some of your awesome Cherokee help right now. I'm so confused, again. Please visit me in my dreams tonight. I love you.

Kissing. I want to kiss Aaron, but I don't want his tongue down my throat. My ex took all he wanted and that was that. I'd never liked a full tongue in my mouth, not with my ex or the guys I dated in school. Never a full tongue thrust at all. Kissing. To me kissing is tender, sweet, gentle, with tongues dancing together, but not full-on tongue. Am I normal? What is the normal? Is half tongue normal? I only know how I feel about kissing. I must Google this and read up on how women feel about it and how a woman wants to be kissed. Then I'd know if I was normal or not.

Those muscular thighs… and a flutter in my stomach… Aaron brings this out in me, a grand desire to watch the muscles he sported flex, and I was in awe of. That flutter I'd felt, sort of like the quickening sensation a pregnant woman feels, yet this flutter pooled warmth within me in my lower belly. Of course, in nursing school, I was taught that sex was meant to be enjoyed by both participants. Did I just classify Aaron and me as participants? Oh my. My last thought as I fell asleep was, *Alexa, find my brain. My brain and my heart are not in sync.*

Chapter Seventeen

Danny

Today was Sunday, and I hoped my mom would take me ice skating in Evergreen today. I loved skating on the lake because the elk were always around. Majestic elk. Huge antlers! An elk herd lived there all year long.

I decided to surprise Mom with breakfast! I wasn't allowed to cook on my own, so I set the table and poured Fruity Pebbles into two bowls with orange juice for us. Mom let me have my favorite cereal one day a week, the other days were cooked bacon and eggs, pancakes, muffins, and ham.

"Mom, wake up please. Mom, I made breakfast!"

"What did you say, Danny?"

"I made a surprise breakfast for us. Come into the kitchen. Please, Mom. I know I can't cook on the stove by myself, but I made us breakfast." Then I ran back into the kitchen.

Mom came in and smiled at me as she looked over

the kitchen table. "Oh, Danny, my sweet and caring boy. What a wonderful surprise! Let me start the coffee maker and grab milk from the fridge."

After we ate most of our breakfast, I asked my mom if we could go skating in Evergreen. Mom said Bel Mar was closer.

I told mom I wanted to see the elk, too, and we might catch an ice hockey game to watch, and those ice fishermen, they are always there when the lake freezes over. "Please, Mom."

Mom gave in and it was a pinky swear deal that today we would skate.

"Danny, would you like for me to call Aaron and see if he and Lisa want to go, too?"

"Yup. That was my next question! You just read my mind, Mom!" Then we both giggled. I knew today would be a truly fun day. Mom called Dr. Aaron and he agreed to go with us to Evergreen. This time Mom planned to drive and told Dr. Aaron to please have Lisa's car seat ready for our Jeep.

Mom picked up Dr. Aaron and Lisa and we set off for Evergreen, only twenty-two miles away. The elk were all over the Heart of Evergreen. We went to the Evergreen Lake House for skate rental. I could see ice fishing tents set up to the east on the snow (ice underneath), and in one area guys played ice hockey on ice that had snow removed. A man was clearing off the snow on the area for skaters. He pushed the snow into banks around the edges of the skate part of the ice.

"Can Lisa skate, Dr. Aaron?" I'd had my skates on first! But I had to wait for Lisa to have help with the skates.

"No, Danny," he said to me, "Lisa is learning how to skate, but must have help."

Soon we were on the ice! Mom skated with me, then kept watch over me like always, as Dr. Aaron and Lisa skated up. I took off and skated a figure eight. Mom yelled that I was awesome, but that was the only fancy skating I could do. I skated for fun. Lisa got tired so my mom, Dr. Aaron and Lisa sat down on an outdoor bench at the lake house with a heat lamp right above.

When I was tired, I glanced up to see Dr. Aaron kissing my mom!!! Whoa! I skated over and my mom said it was time to leave, as a lot of people were on the ice now. I wanted to ask about that kiss I know I saw, but I stayed quiet, and listened to them talk on the way back to Lookout Mountain. After dropping off Dr. Aaron and Lisa, we went home.

Now was my time, and I was going to find out about that kiss! "Mom, I saw you and Dr. Aaron kiss! Will you get married? Will we be a *real* family?"

"Danny, I love Aaron and Lisa both, and we all belong together. Marriage is a huge step. Now, don't get excited but, Aaron proposed to me right in the Heart of Evergreen, and I said yes."

"Show me your ring!" I squealed with delight.

"I don't have one yet, Danny. Aaron plans to take me out to choose the ring I want. It will be more than six months before we can marry as steps are involved and I want to be sure we do the right thing."

"Yippee!" I shouted and my mom asked me to calm down.

That night, I dreamed of having a dad and a little sister.

Chapter Eighteen

Aaron

Wow. Sarah agreed to marry me, with conditions. A lot of conditions, but each one had merit and made sense. Sarah looked out for all four of us.

First, we agreed that our love was honest and true, and we would continue to build our love on our great foundation of friendship. We were totally ahead of the game in this department. Deep friendship is a solid base for marriage. During this time, Sarah wanted to make sure we were compatible.

Second, as Sarah pointed out, we'd not had sex, yet, and there was much to discuss. Discussion came first. Back to the sex part later.

Third, Sarah wanted a church wedding, and not just any church wedding. Sarah wanted us to marry in the Catholic faith we shared. My love wanted to marry at St. Mary Queen of the Universe, a church we both were members of, and this meant we would meet with our priest multiple times to discuss marriage, how to work out differences, and we had to get annulments. Appointment made for both of us.

First, we informed our priest that we'd decided to get married. Then we talked with Father Barry, about the annulment process. In the Catholic church an annulment "is a legal ruling that erases a marriage by declaring the marriage null and void and that the union was never legally valid." This meant that the church didn't see our prior marriages as legal in the eyes of the Catholic church. However, "even if the marriage is erased, the marriage records remain on file." Father Barry said that a religious annulment is *not* a legal dissolution of a civil marriage. There is a difference. A huge difference.

For Sarah, the annulment process would go faster as the church took into consideration the fact that Sarah hadn't married in the church nor had the marriage been blessed in the church. Let alone the abuse she sustained and the countless rapes that happened. Therefore, Sarah would be entitled to receive an annulment. Sarah was concerned and asked if having a marriage annulled would make Danny illegitimate. That thought had not even entered my mind! I was impressed yet again with how amazing my woman was and how Father Barry said that it's "a common misconception that an annulment makes children illegitimate in church law, and that it was a false belief." Furthermore, a Catholic annulment is a separate process from a civil divorce, but the Church would ask if the civil obligations had been fulfilled. Since the three of us were together, Sarah explained to Father Barry how the marriage happened, when and where, and the abuse and suffering that Sarah, Danny, and Simon endured. Danny was NOT considered illegitimate, and Sarah was satisfied.

Neither one of my marriages occurred in the Catholic church, so my annulments happened just as easily. Mine had not been blessed in the church, either. Lisa would NOT be considered illegitimate. I cringed at the word. Damn… No child should ever have that label, no matter how their birth came about. My first wife up and left me, and my second wife left me right after Lisa was born. Neither wife had fulfilled the civil obligations of marriage.

Then we discussed dates for getting married. Sarah figured that we could have a late July wedding, if everything worked out. Plus, we would have to wait six months from the time we informed Father Barry of our intentions to get married as that was the way of Catholicism. We thanked Father Barry for the guidance he gave us.

My Sarah figured this time frame would help us build upon our connection, and with both children as a family unit. We blended, we meshed. My mom and Cindy were happy for both of us. I was glad Cindy had come around and was normal again.

I took Sarah to the finest jeweler in the city. Together we looked at wedding rings. Sarah didn't want a large engagement diamond and wedding band, so we looked until the rings were found. Sarah chose a beautiful yellow gold ring with a moderate sized engagement diamond in the middle and wrapped with a swirl of smaller diamonds. The matching band sported the same wrapped swirl of smaller diamonds and the two rings fit together perfectly. The set spoke to Sarah. My ring was easy to find, a nice yellow gold band with etchings and small diamonds on the top of the band.

I can't wait to marry Sarah. I also wanted to make love right then and there, to show Sarah my full love, yet that was a work in progress for my soon-to-be wife.

Chapter Nineteen

Sarah

Time flew by fast, as in one half blink of an eye.

Aaron and I were required to attend an Engaged Encounter Weekend, which was a Catholic teaching course for couples. Ours was held in March at an old stone monastery in Denver proper.

Women slept on one side of an upstairs floor, the men in a separate area upstairs and no mingling of couples allowed. Neither were kids allowed. The purpose of this couple's retreat was to ensure that we allowed time to discuss important issues early in our engagement and focus on our future marriage without the distractions of life and wedding details.

Each couple had to stay the entire weekend, and if someone arrived late or left early, important aspects would be missed, thus no certificate of completion of the retreat. Essentially, the purpose of the Catholic Engaged Encounter weekend was to interact with and talk with your fiancé about issues you may not have already discussed. This was important to us both. Two married couples ran the retreat, and our mentors' incorporated presentations, self-reflection, and couple's dialogue.

Among our discussions, we talked about family—family traditions and values we grew up with influenced our expectations for marriage.

We discussed sacrament—a sacramental marriage in the Catholic Church is a lifetime covenant. Marriage was not to be entered into lightly.

Communication—each couple had to understand that good verbal and non-verbal communication was the key to a strong marriage. During discussion, we added that a strong base of friendship to build our communication and marriage upon was essential in our case, and the mentors added that part into their future teaching. *Score another point!*

Intimacy was involved. For any couple, growing to know your soon-to-be spouse more deeply included emotional, intellectual, physical, and spiritual intimacy. This was a work in progress for me. I wanted Aaron, I wanted Aaron to make love to me, but I had a few hurdles to jump first. I knew Aaron would be gentle, but I saw my body as totally imperfect, and I wondered if my body would respond to his touch the way most women talked about in their own lives. I still felt like 'damaged goods.'

Lastly, values were discussed. It's essential that couples have common values, and for us, we did.

Our Engaged Encounter Weekend was a huge benefit for us, and all the couples who attended as well as our mentors.

Chapter Twenty

Aaron

The months flew by. Mom and Cindy wanted to help with the wedding planning, but Sarah knew what she wanted, a small gathering of close friends and family, and a Catholic maid of honor. I wanted my best man, Eric, a fellow doctor, at my side. He wasn't Catholic, but only one person was required to be Catholic for us to marry. We didn't need or want bridesmaids or groomsmen, and Sarah thought that Lisa would be a perfect flower girl and Danny the ring bearer. This small wedding was exactly what I had in mind, too. My mom and sister, Cindy, didn't do much as Sarah had it all under control, and my love was still a bit nervous of Cindy. Sarah kindly asked Cindy if being a lector for the wedding was acceptable, Cindy replied in the affirmative, and so my sister was part of the ceremony. Sarah and I chose the Bible passages we wanted to have read during our ceremony.

In May, we decided to combine our households into one. We still hadn't had sex yet, so we weren't 'living in sin,' but Sarah wanted to do this to make sure the four of us meshed as well as things had been prior to now. Sarah and Danny moved into my home on Lookout Mountain, and each had one of the large bedroom suites. Danny had his room arranged with his own *Cars* bedding and his toys and posters, and I bought a lit curio cabinet for his derby car and trophies as I thought they shouldn't get damaged, and more might be added to the collection later.

Sarah left her room the way it was and simply personalized it with paintings and pieces she'd cross-stitched, music, framed photographs, and books. Sarah loved books.

Late one evening in June, with both kids fast asleep, Sarah and I had just finished watching a 'chick flick.' I didn't want to break up our cuddle time together when suddenly, Sarah looked up at me. Those pink lips, I must kiss them.

We kissed tenderly and gently as before, but this time Sarah pressed for more. Our tongues danced together in that age old rhythm, only half tongue, not full-to-your-throat. Sarah hated full-on throat kissing and so did I. I sighed as I could kiss Sarah 24/7. I knew my arms were designed to specifically hold Sarah. That beautiful slender body pressed against me, and I was lost. Wrapped in each other's arms and our hands running lightly over each other, I gently cupped a breast. Sarah froze!

"I'm sorry, Sarah. I got carried away," I whispered as I continued to hold the woman of my dreams. At the same time, I slung curse words at Sarah's ex. *Blast that scumbag of a man!*

Sarah moaned, then looked down and said, "I'm sorry. It's my body. I'm scared I won't be good enough for you. I don't want my body compared to all the other bodies of women you take care of. I'm a nurse, I see men's bodies, but I simply take care of my patient, rarely do I appreciate any muscular form. As a doctor, you see females, many with perfect to-die-for bodies. Men are different, the visuals stay with you. I'm ashamed of my body, and I don't want to disappoint. But I also need the man I will marry. I love your body, what I've seen of it, and I'm sure the rest of your body is fine. My love for you isn't built on how you look, you know that. But still, men are visual creatures, and I..."

I wiped away the tears and hugged Sarah tightly. "Let's take it slow, Sarah. We can stop at any time. I promise to be gentle, and I adore your body. I want to show you my love, and I want you to tell me to stop when you can't continue. Why don't we go to my bedroom for complete privacy so neither child will walk in on us?"

Sarah nodded yes, and we went to my bedroom. I kept the lights off so that Sarah could undress and get into my bed without me seeing the nakedness my fiancé was ashamed of. I knew darkness was the only way for my Sarah to start out on our sexual life together.

Slowly I removed my own clothes and slid in next to Sarah. My love didn't shy away from me. *Curse that vile creature of a man who'd done horrible things to my fiancé.* Surprisingly, Sarah slipped over closer to me. This was the biggest hurdle for us to get through.

"I want to give you a rundown on my body, Aaron. From top to bottom, and I don't want to hear words from you until I'm finished. Agreed?"

"Yes, Sarah, tell me the fears and feelings begging to come out. Only then can I help to heal you, my love."

"Well, my hair and my face, I'm okay with all of that. But my body is far from perfect. My breasts are not the same size, and they are small. I have one scar between my breasts that happened when I was nine years old. My mother made sure a beauty mark was removed, probably out of spite. At the same time, a benign tumor was removed from directly under my left nipple, so I have a scar around that nipple."

Sarah continued to knock down each physical part of herself. I listened to all the fears and how she'd been destroyed, the numerous exploratory surgeries she'd had, and all the insecurities within Sarah gushed out, between small cries and whimpers. Sarah kept knocking down numerous faults, and I encouraged my love to speak freely, to tell me the pain of the past and the dreams for the future we would share. Finally at an end, I nuzzled the swan-like neck of my woman.

"Can I tell you what I see, Sarah?" My love nodded yes. "I see a beautiful and sensual woman. I see a woman who had been hurt, but also a woman who will heal through me." I followed that with extreme intimate breathing behind each ear, the most sensual experience she'd never experienced in the past. The moans elicited intensified my own.

"I see two breasts, one a bit smaller than the other, but most women usually have a slightly larger left breast," I reminded her, as I nuzzled each breast in turn, gently ravishing attention on both. "The way I see it, is I get to have two sizes to enjoy. Your breasts are not small. Your breasts are rounded in a gorgeous way and your nipples are pert and perky, too." Then I gently suckled each breast as Sarah moaned louder.

Slowly, I moved lower on Sarah's body, kissing, and teasing her flat abdomen and the scars displayed. I cared not about the scars, nor the stretch marks, so I kissed each one. Sarah cried out.

"Are you okay?" I asked as I nuzzled a bit lower.

"Yes, Aaron, I'm okay, but no one ever kissed my body like you did just now."

"All of the things I'm doing, Sarah, are normal when couples are in love. I won't hurt you or thrust myself upon you, ever."

My fingers went lower and played at Sarah's moist core and womanhood. Sarah moaned louder and I could tell it was enjoyable. I certainly loved every bit of our love making. Then I had to do it. I could not stop. I lowered my face into the core of the woman I loved. Sarah became rigid immediately. I stopped. "What's wrong, Sweetheart?"

"I'm nervous, a little bit scared, and ashamed. Do you really want to do that to me? Down there? No one ever did this to me before. You're my first, Aaron. My scent, my taste, do you like it? I mean, really do you like it?"

"Ambrosia—pure Nectar of the Gods. Don't worry, we have time, and I love you and your body. Let me love you the way you deserve." With that, I lowered my head between her thighs and used my tongue, teasing the womanhood and ravishing my Sarah gently. Sarah cried out and then, my love gushed. I lapped it all up.

Finally, I entered and thrust gently, until Sarah demanded more. I did Sarah's bidding. I was lost, Sarah the same. Lost in each other. Afterwards, Sarah cried.

"What's wrong, Sarah? Tell me the truth because I plan on loving you until you believe the truth about your body."

"I love you, Aaron. You're the first to love me in this way."

"I love you too, Honey Bunny," I promised as we snuggled together and slowly fell asleep. I thought about how *I was the first to teach Sarah how making love was truly meant to be, I was the FIRST.*

Chapter Twenty-One

Danny

May…

I loved being at Aaron's house. You read that right! Aaron told me it was time to use Aaron and not Dr Aaron. How about that? My soon to be new dad wanted me to use Aaron!

School was almost out for the summer. Mom was called to be present for a meeting at school with my teacher, my principal, and my special reading teacher. I was nervous, but Mom told me everything would be fine. I did have a good year with my grades. So, I decided not to worry.

Sarah…

I attended the IEP meeting. Danny's principal appeared rather nervous. I was informed that my child's 'label' had been changed. Imagine that…. Danny was now labeled LD- Learning Disabled due to problems with reading and reading comprehension. The principal still couldn't get the word Educably spelled correctly.

The IEP will assist Danny all through school and into college.

In passing, that man had the gall to casually mention that "we were wrong to have had Danny repeat first grade." I stared Danny's principal down, then stated, "Try listening to the child and the child's parent next time. The bullying Danny received never had to be. Danny need not have suffered. Furthermore, it isn't educably but educable, so get your damn spelling right!" Then I walked away.

Danny…

Mom told me that I get to go to second grade in the fall! I get to keep my special reading teacher, which is great because I love all my teachers. I hope the kids don't pick on me in second grade. Soon, no school for the summer! I get to take swimming lessons again! How awesome is that! Mom will marry Aaron this summer, too! I will get a dad and a sister!

Chapter Twenty-Two

Sarah

Grandma Cordie, this is what you wanted for me. Your wisdom is strong and true. Aaron is strong and true. We are truly meant to be. Cordie, your Cherokee spirit gave me endurance to take a leap of faith. Thank you, Grandma.

July came up fast! Danny was awesome with the swimming lessons, my son a fish in water. Danny and Lisa were already siblings in action and spoken word. My heart was happy to hear and see the beauty of both children so happy.

Soon, I would walk down the aisle to meet my beloved at the end. Aaron didn't care for the color mauve, yet all he wanted was to get married and I chose the colors I wanted with an 80s and 90s vibe. My colors of pink, mauve, light grey, and white fit me and the small wedding to a perfect T.

Money wasn't an issue at all, but Aaron and I

wanted an intimate wedding with family and some close friends. The guest list was full at forty people, and that number included both kids, Aaron, and me. Talk about not many people in a huge church for a wedding! Neither of us cared to have a wedding dance, or any of the hoopla that surrounds many weddings. The invitations read 'No wedding gifts please, rather donate to your favorite charity.' This wedding was to fit four hearts into one big heart!

A wedding photographer was hired, and two cousins were tasked with usher duty, and of course, Cindy was lector. One cousin was the organist and another one sang. Jill, another nurse, and co-worker friend, created a perfect three-tier white cake with white frosting and topped with pink satin bells decorated with tiny roses, baby's breath, and Chantilly lace, created by me! I loved decorating the bride and groom flute glasses, and a lovely unity candle I'd decorated with a lot of pearl pins and placed upon a cut crystal base. A perfect, intimate wedding.

The afternoon before our wedding, a gathering space at the church was set up for the reception and all the tables covered in white tablecloths with candle and floral centerpieces I'd created. Sadie oversaw all of this.

I was a creative person, so I'd chosen not to have a florist do any of the flowers. I created my floral pieces with silk flowers, and I created every bouquet, boutonniere, corsage, and a small flower bouquet for Mary, the mother of Jesus. I also decided to make all the headpieces and my veil. I needed one fitting for my wedding dress as did Suzy, my matron of honor.

Today was *the* day! Aaron and I would get married today. Was I nervous? Not a bit, I knew my man. Suzy was with me as I got ready. Lisa sat next to me and Aaron's mom, Alice and sister, Cindy both helped as well.

My dress…

I wore a gorgeous white, silk satin mermaid style dress with a sweetheart neckline, and short puff silk satin sleeves. My dress fit like a glove, the bodice and skirt covered in Chantilly lace and small pearls. My skirt hugged my hips, and my hem was a flouncy high-low silky hem—no lace, higher in the front than the back, and no train—I didn't want one. My dress wasn't a traditional mermaid style dress, but the one on me screamed Sarah! I wore white satin shoes, white pantyhose, and a pink silk and white lace garter tucked away for Aaron to find later. A matching white lace quarter cut under bust corset with pink accents completed my 'underneath the dress' details.

My long, blonde curly hair was pulled to one side high on my head and secured in place with cascading curls flowing down the opposite side. I'd covered my silk hat with Chantilly lace, tiny white roses, and baby's breath. A matching veil completed my head piece.

My matron of honor, Suzy, gave me an antique gold cameo necklace for my 'something old and borrowed,' I wore new pearl stud earrings Aaron gifted to me, and I wrapped my blue rosary in among my bridal bouquet of pink, white, and mauve roses, orchids, mixed greenery, and baby's breath that cascaded downwards with pink and mauve ribbons.

Suzy wore a pink silk satin midi dress with a sweetheart neckline and cap sleeves. She also wore pink satin shoes, a white and pink rose hair piece with baby's breath adorned her short black hair. I made a bouquet like mine, yet smaller, for Suzy, and I gifted my matron of honor with a gorgeous graduated and twisted triple strand freshwater pearl necklace.

Lisa wore a cute, soft pink satin dress overlaid with Chantilly lace, and a flower crown of pink roses and baby's breath mixed with greenery. White tights and white shoes completed the outfit.

My dad's brother, John, gave me away. Dad would have approved, and I'm sure my dad watched from Heaven. As I walked down the aisle with Uncle John, I saw my true love. Aaron stood next to the best man, Michael—Aaron's best friend and a doctor. They both wore light grey/silver tuxedoes with pink cummerbunds and pink rose boutonnieres, made by me, of course.

Danny was a perfect 'mini-me' to Aaron in a matching tuxedo and boutonniere.

The children walked down the aisle first, followed by Suzy, then Uncle John and me.

Chapter Twenty-Three

Aaron

Sarah was perfect and more than creative. My girl was headed towards me down the aisle and soon to be my wife.

After the wedding, the photographer took photographs. Never in my wildest dreams did I expect what happened next.

Group pictures were taken and suddenly, Cindy called out for a family photograph of 'just the Leawood's.' Cindy told Danny that he was not 'family, not a Leawood, therefore Danny can't be in the Leawood's only group photographs.' Neither Sarah nor I heard this exchange as it was a busy time with the photographer.

During the reception later, I found Danny crying and he refused to talk to me. I took Danny over to sit by Sarah and he cried harder. Finally, having been soothed by Sarah, Danny spoke.

"Cindy said I wasn't a Leawood and that I wasn't a part of the Leawood family. I wasn't allowed to be in the pictures with the Leawood's only." Danny sobbed uncontrollably. Sarah and I were shocked. Cindy was too toxic! This had to stop right now!

Shoulders shaking, Danny cried out, "You married Aaron, Mom, and I'm not family. Simon was taken away from me and now… now you are, too. I'm alone with no family! I'm alone in the world! I have no one!" as the words tore at Sarah's heart and mine.

My mom came over to see what the problem was, and Danny told my mother everything. Mom was appalled, yet somehow it wasn't a total surprise.

While Sarah and Alice comforted Danny, and a crying Lisa by then, I took Cindy to task, and right in front of Sarah, my mom, and both kids.

"Cindy, Danny is a Leawood whether Anderson or Leawood is Danny's last name. He is MY son! Danny will always be *my* son! This will *never* change! Leave now or I will call the police. You will *never* hurt my family, again, ever! I don't want you within 100 yards of my family! Do you understand?" Cindy left with a smile.

After Cindy left, I sat down with Danny and had a heart-to-heart talk.

"Danny, family isn't always blood or marriage related. Family is those who you love, and I love you. You are not alone. You have a lot of family. Even Sadie is your family. Alice is your grandma," I explained as Danny hugged me tightly and wouldn't let go.

"Mom, this changes things. We can't let Danny and Lisa stay with you in Springs while we are on our honeymoon." And Sarah nodded in agreement.

"Aaron, I would feel better, and so would the children, if we postponed our honeymoon for now. After this fiasco, the children need both you and me now, and I think Alice needs you, too."

Watching Mom's face closely I asked, "Are you okay living with Cindy? At 73, Cindy can take advantage of you easily. Has Cindy hurt you or abused you in any way?"

Sighing, Alice replied, "I'm exhausted Aaron. Cindy demands too much work out of me in the coffee shop. I've been afraid to tell you. The condo belongs to Cindy, as you know." Mom's eyes welled with unshed tears.

"Mom, Cindy is too toxic to the four of us and

you. Sarah and I feel that Danny and Lisa were traumatized by the events with the photographer. This was planned long ago by Cindy."

Glancing at my wife, I added, "Mom, think about this. Come and live with us. We have the room and I'm happy to build a mother-in-law house near Sadie's. You could invite your friends over and the kids wouldn't be underfoot all the time. I know you would love the local book club, and the meetings and literary discussions are what you lived for in the past, after dad passed away. You deserve to enjoy the rest of the life the Lord has given you and have quality time with Danny and Lisa. My housekeeper, Sadie, has been lonely lately and the two of you love each other as family. Please come and live with us. Please say yes."

"I will, Aaron. You know I love your home, and I can finally see my grandchildren as much as I want to. Cindy had me so worked up. I got no rest and I'm exhausted. That's why I've lost weight, Sarah. Cindy is bitter and… thank you, Sarah. You knew, you could tell. I see that now! You are the kind of daughter I've always wanted. Aright, Aaron, yes. Thank you." With arms around each grandchild, Mom told them of the plans made and asked Danny to use the name Grandma like Lisa does. The kids squealed with delight. Danny's torture from Cindy was over. Healing could now begin for each of us.

Chapter Twenty-Four

Sarah

Aaron loved removing my white lace panties, pink silk and white lace garter, and my matching white lace quarter cut under bust corset with pink accents, after he took a couple of photographs! Men! Aaron's appeal came from a confidence he exuded without ego, and I loved my husband dearly.

Love, learning to love and to be cherished for the first time. Aaron does that and more, and I reciprocated back.

Thank you, Lord Jesus. You are so good to me.

Epilogue....

Danny...

"**I** became an Eagle Scout! I went to college. I also work with high tech expensive machining centers for an aerospace company in Los Angeles, not bad for "Educably Mentally Handicapped." My blended family was awesome. I could not ask for a better dad, mom, sister, and grandma."

Sarah....

"**I**'d hoped for love once and I'd found it. Thank you, Jesus!"

Aaron...

"**S**arah was the perfect match for me, our family, and they are my number one priority."

Alice and Sadie…

"We became deep friends and were always there for each other. I'd finally found peace, away from Cindy.

Biography

Mary L. Schmidt writes under the name of S. Jackson along with her husband Michael, pen name A Raymond. She grew up in a small Kansas (USA) town and lived in more than one state since then. At this time, Ms. Schmidt and her husband split their time between Kansas and Colorado (they love the mountains and off road 4-wheeling). Traveling is one of their most favorite things to do and she always has a book or even three books that to read, in the same week. Books have always been her thing. It seemed like every time she turned around, a new library card was needed due to the current one being stamped complete. Diving into a good book made any day perfect and you would be surprised at the number of books she has read over and over. She drew paper dolls and clothes for them, and using watercolor as her medium when painting scenes, especially flowers. She continued with art in high school exploring a wide variety of arts and loved it! Her creative side loves to be an amateur "shutter-bug" and they have an online art gallery. In college, she went into the sciences of all things and received a bachelor's degree in the Science of Nursing. Her nursing career was highly successful, and she hung up her nursing hat in December 2012.

S. Jackson is a retired registered nurse; a member of the Catholic Church and has taught kindergarten Catechism; she has worked in various capacities for The American Cancer Society, March of Dimes, Cub and Boy Scouts, (son, Gene, is an Eagle Scout), and sponsored trips for high school music children. She loves all forms of art but mostly focuses on the visual arts, such as amateur photography, traditional, and graphic art as her health allows.

She has written more than 30 books with five more in various stages of production, and she is included in four anthologies.

A. Raymond is a member of the Catholic Church and has helped his wife with The American Cancer Society, March of Dimes, Cub and Boy Scouts, and sponsored children alongside his wife on music trips. He devotes his spare time to fishing, reading, playing poker, Jeeping, and travel adventures with his wife. Spending time with their grandson, Austin, and granddaughter, Emma, happens to be another favorite past time.

Other Books

Sammy
Hero At Age Five
"..point of view of a five-year-old boy ..main focus ..is to relay the love he has for his family and how grateful he was to spend every minute he could with them."
When Angels Fly
S. Jackson
A. Raymond
"I cried, got angry, and cheered throughout this book – it is touching, heartbreaking, difficult, powerful, and loving, all at once. Wow – what a powerful book!"
~ Monica

Links

"Love the parent and educator guide in the back. Teach your child good touch/bad touch, and body ownership!"

"Take a stand today and build up your child's self-esteem! Stop bullies and child suicide!"

Available at Amazon, Walmart, and All Bookstores!